WIZDOM

FOREVER YOUR GANGSTA

NAI

U.A.D PRESENTS

STAY UP TO DATE

To stay up to date on new releases, plus get information on contests, sneak peeks and more,

Click the link below...
https://mailchi.mp/6d21003686d1/subscribe

SOUNDTRACKS

Scan the QR Code below to listen to the Soundtracks/Singles of some of your favorite U.A.D titles:

Don't have Spotify or Apple Music?
No Sweat!
Visit your choice streaming platform and search URBAN AINT DEAD.

Currently on lock serving a bid?
JPay, iHeartRadio, WHATEVER!
We got you covered.
Simply log into your facility's kiosk or tablet, go to music and
search URBAN AINT DEAD.

U.A.D PRESENTS

Like & Follow us on social media:

FB - URBAN AINT DEAD

IG: @uadpresents

Tik Tok - @uadpresents

Submission Guidelines

Submit the first three chapters of your completed manuscript to urbanaintdead@gmail.com, subject line: Your book's title. The manuscript must be in a .doc file and sent as an attachment. The document should be in Times New Roman, double-spaced, and in size 12 font. Also, provide your synopsis and full contact information. If sending multiple submissions, they must each be in a separate email. Have a story but no way to submit it electronically? You can still submit to URBAN AINT DEAD. Send in the first three chapters, written or typed, of your completed manuscript to:

URBAN AINT DEAD
P.O Box 448
Maybrook, NY 12543

DO NOT send original manuscript. Must be a duplicate.
Provide your synopsis and a cover letter containing your full contact information.
Thanks for considering URBAN AINT DEAD.

Previously In "Seizing A Gangsta's Heart For The Summer"

"I don't know where we go from here but know that you're safe with me. We've uncovered some shit about each other this past week, and I'm open to doing more of that to build on solid ground. And I know that shit that your ex pulled isn't something you're gonna heal from after three weeks. So long as you're willing to give me a fair chance, I wanna explore this. You good with that?"

I heard his words and smiled big. "Yeah, I'm good with that." We sealed the new journey with a kiss.

"And I'll still put a hole in that nigga at any given time. You just say the word."

"Oh, my God! Shut up, crazy."

"Let's eat, beautiful." Slapping my butt, he grabbed my hand and led me into the dining room to join the rest of the crew.

How I managed to get rid of a dog ass nigga and lock down a gangsta in the matter of three weeks was a mystery to me, but my mama always said, "Good things come to the persistent," and Wiz was a persistent one.

IT'S 12:45. IT'S 95 DEGREES. I GOT A NEW NIGGA & MY NEW NIGGA GOT ME!

Y'ALL ASKED FOR MORE... WELL, HERE IT GO!

1

—

ALACEA

rina's *I Got A Thang For You* echoed throughout my room as my phone rang in the middle of the night. Knowing who the ringtone had been specifically assigned to, a smile instantly spread across my face. Rolling over, I picked up the phone and answered on speaker.

"Hey, baby," I greeted Wizdom through a yawn. **"You on your way?"**

Our routine for the last few months had been for him to call me when his night ended. Aware of Wizdom's position in the streets, I liked to hear his voice before he went to sleep. It gave me solace to know when he made it in safe, whether he was going home or coming to my place. Tonight, his destination was my house.

"Yeah, beautiful. You can put the call on speaker and go back to sleep."

"It's on speaker, baby. You hungry?" I'd just fallen asleep not too long ago, awaiting his arrival. My eyes were still closed as he spoke, but I was alert.

"I'm good, bae. I don't want you up burning shit on my

behalf." I imagined his goofy smile over the phone as he snickered.

"**I was referring to heating up some leftovers with a side of coochie. But if you not hungry, who am I to force feed you?**"

"**Ooooh,**" he let out. "**I need the pussy, beautiful. That shit like melatonin. I tell my mama it's pussytonin.**"

"**Wizdom! I know you don't be talkin' to your mother about my coochie.**"

"**I talk to my moms about almost everything, beautiful. That's my dawg. She's been complimenting me on how well rested I look. I just attribute it to that good stuff between your thighs amongst other things.**"

Giggling, I placed the phone next to my head and turned on my side. "**Something is wrong with you. How long before you get here?**" I yawned again as I stretched.

"**About six minutes. What you got on?**"

"**My skin.**"

"**Ooouuu, see, this why I fuck witchu the way I do. You always keep a nigga in mind.**"

"**You silly. How was your day?**"

"**Productive. I made it another day above ground, so I'm grateful.**"

"**Me too.**"

Since becoming an item, I'd been enjoying every minute of him. Wizdom made me feel like I was the only woman in the world, and I never got tired of hearing him call me beautiful. He'd transitioned from bachelor to someone's man – my man. And in that transition, I felt like I knew more about him than I ever cared to ask about Quan. Just thinking about Quan made me thankful that I'd dodged that bullet. I'd let that situation go on longer than I cared to admit, but had it not been for his bullshit and careless-ness, I wouldn't have had the space to even entertain

Wizdom. I still couldn't believe that nigga had a baby on me.

"**Beautiful, you sleeping?**"

"**No, baby. I'm getting up, so I can heat you up some food.**" Pulling the sheet off my naked body, I reached for the robe that laid at the edge of my bed.

"**Aye, beautiful. I appreciate you wanting to feed a nigga, but don't you put yo' pussy near that stove. You burn Fat Ma, and I'll never forgive you.**"

"**Wizdom!**" I cackled. "**I'm putting on a robe. What is wrong witchu?**"

"**Nothing. You said you was feeding me some of that good stuff. I'm just making sure she straight.**"

"**Boy, hush. I'm gonna heat up the shrimp linguine I made earlier. It's going in the microwave.**" Sliding my feet into my slippers, I shook my head.

I could always count on him to have something crazy to say out his mouth every few seconds.

"**Oh, aight. In that case, leave the robe. You gon' feed me my food?**"

"**Yes. On a fork,**" I replied, snickering, setting the robe back down.

"**Beautiful.**"

"**No, Wizdom. I said that was a one-time thing. I still can't believe I did that.**"

"**You do a lot when you off that Patron, baby.**"

"**Well, I'm very sober.**" I blushed and stood up from the bed.

"**The food tastes better when it's from your mouth though.**" His tone was low, making me squeeze my thighs together and rethink my no.

Wizdom wanting to eat food out of my mouth was crazy, but I let him do it once on a drunk night. It was so weird, but after the first couple bites, I said fuck it. He was right. That Patron was a motherfucka.

"You so nasty. Did you eat at all today?" I changed the subject, knowing he only had a few more words before convincing me to do as he wanted.

"Yeah. Breakfast earlier. You know I'm usually on the go, so eating is the last thing on my mind when I'm grindin'."

"Am I on your mind when you're out grindin'?" Judging from our daily conversations, I had an idea of what his answer would be, but like a woman, I wanted to hear him verbally express it.

"I think about you all day. The call log in my phone is proof of that."

A wide grin spread across my face, and my heart galloped. "Awww, you make me feel like I'm that girl when you talk to me like that. I mean, I knew I was the shit, but you make sure to remind me."

"And I don't plan on stopping. I'm pulling onto your street now."

"Okay. Park in the garage next to my truck. I'm putting your plate in the microwave."

"Cool. I'll be up in a minute. Gimme kiss."

I made kissing sounds into the phone and hung up. I didn't mind getting out of bed at two in the morning to fix a plate for Wizdom or even give him some pussy. A man who was gentle, patient, honest, considerate, and selfless, all while keepin' shit gangsta, deserved five-course meals and an endless amount of cooch. His actions made me want to go the extra mile for him. Wizdom took his time with me, understanding that I was fresh out of a toxic relationship that almost swallowed me whole. The reassurance was top tier and much appreciated.

As I made my way into the kitchen, dressed in nothing per his request, I flicked on the light and caught a glimpse of myself in the stainless-steel fridge. The last I checked, I'd gained about fifteen pounds over the past few months. Happy weight of course. And it went to the right places, my thighs and hips. I even noticed a small pudge, but I loved every bit of it, and Wizdom couldn't keep his eyes or hands off me. My man made it known how sexy I was from the moment I opened my eyes in the morning to the time I closed them at night – as he the fuck should.

I admired my curves for a few seconds before continuing with the task at hand. The microwave dinged at the same time I heard keys in the door. Taking the plate out and placing it on the counter, I went in the fridge to get him something to drink to have with his dinner and late-night snack.

"Damn, baby. I can see that pussy from the back." I heard him say from behind me.

Giggling inwardly, I leaned farther into the fridge and spread my legs wide to give a better view. "What about now?" I asked, peeking between my legs.

Licking his full lips, he took slow steps toward me. "Can I have my dessert now?" he questioned, caressing my booty lovingly.

Wiz had big, firm, manly hands, yet they were soft when he touched me. As he squeezed my cheeks, I let out a low moan.

"Yes, baby. You can have me," I cooed softly.

"Close the fridge, put your hands on the counter, left leg up there too." His directions were precise, and I followed them to a T.

The growl in his tone made my pussy leak in anticipation. Whether it was his tongue or the dick first, I knew I was sure to be more than satisfied. Tooting my round ass in the air with my leg up, I looked back at him.

"Like this?"

"Mmhmm, just like that. One second, beautiful." Turning to the sink, he quickly washed his hands and dried them before giving my ass a hard smack.

The man was even mindful of my PH balance. I'd be damned

if I didn't get lockjaw on account of all the dick suckin' I planned to do.

"Sssss," I hissed at the stinging while my clit thumped at the same time.

Standing directly behind me, he kissed my neck tenderly, then my shoulder blade, trailing his fingers around my waist, down my pelvis, and stopping at my wet mound.

"She's warm for me," he spoke in between kisses. "This pussy always warm for Dada. She miss a nigga?"

The warmth of his mouth against my skin made the hairs on my arms stand up. "Yes, baby," I vocalized through heavy breaths as he slid two fingers inside of me.

"Wet ass pussy," he growled, pulling both fingers out of me and placing them up to my mouth. "Taste her."

Parting my lips, I stuck my tongue out and licked my juices off each one. "Mmmm."

"That's what I be tryna tell you, beautiful. You look good, taste good, and feel even better. And you so obedient when you give it to me. Dada gon' take care of it every time, you hear me?"

The way he spoke had me in a trance, and all I could do was nod. Pushing me forward so that my bare chest was on the counter, the coolness of the marble countertop made my nipples stiffen. As one hand gripped my waist, I could feel him slide into me inch by inch.

"Fuuckk, Wizdommm," I dragged, shuddering as he filled me up.

"Damn, beautiful. You hear that pussy talkin' to me?"

The slapping sounds of my ass meeting his pelvis could be heard throughout the kitchen as he dug into me something serious.

"Yesssss, nigga. Do that shit. Ouuuu. You gon' make me cummm!"

Grabbing me by my neck, he pulled my head back so that his lips were touching my ear. "Where you wanna cum at, beautiful?

Huh? You taking that dick so good. It's your world. What you wanna do? You wanna wet this dick up, or you want me to suck on that clit till it swell up and you rain down on my tongue?"

"Ughhh, Wizdom, shitt!" He rotated his hips to tap at my g-spot, and that little move did the trick. "I'm cummin'!!!" I yelped.

Sinking his teeth in my neck, he played with my clit, pumping in and out of me feverishly. "Goddamn, I'm right there, beautiful. Bounce that ass and get this nut."

I bounced my ass up and down on his dick, cummin' once more with him reaching his peak at the same time. Both spent, we leaned over the counter, panting.

"If I wasn't on birth control, that performance would've been the one to get me pregnant," I joked, tilting my head to kiss him.

"Whenever you ready to retire them pills, you just say the word." Running his tongue across my lips, he slid out of me and placed my leg back down on the floor.

I stayed silent at his statement. I wanted children, but after having experienced two miscarriages, the most traumatic one not long ago, I wasn't sure if I wanted to have that conversation outside of playful banter.

"You go shower, and I'll reheat your food."

"Aight. Thank you, beautiful. I'ma need that again after I eat. You know, just to help me go to sleep faster." Smacking my ass, he winked and walked out of the kitchen.

Just call me Princess Imani Izzi because it was "whatever he liked."

<hr>

THE SUNLIGHT CREPT THROUGH MY CURTAINS, AND I FELT MYSELF snuggled under Wizdom's muscular frame. His legs were wrapped around mine, and his arms held my waist protectively, while our fingers interlocked. I'd become accustomed to sleeping this way since our first overnight stay – close and holding hands throughout the night as if someone would somehow break in and pull us apart. Ughhh, I lived for the physical touch.

Rubbing my thumb over his knuckles, I lifted his hand and kissed the back of it, causing him to stir a little. I shifted slightly, careful not to disturb his sleep, but his grip on my waist tightened, letting me know he wasn't as sleep as he pretended to be. "You up?"

Clearing his throat, he murmured, "I am now that you tryna sneak out the bed."

Laughing softly, I turned, rolling onto my side to face him. His eyes cracked open enough to see my full smile. "Good morning, handsome face."

"Good morning, beautiful." Nuzzling my neck, he exhaled into my skin. "How'd you sleep?"

"The same way I sleep whenever you're in bed with me – like a baby."

Pulling back from my neck, he kissed my forehead then my lips. "Must be that dickadryl."

"Dicka what?"

"Dickadryl. Like that Benadryl our parents used to give us to lowkey put us to sleep. I gave you that dickadryl this morning. Come on, bae. Keep up."

"Wizdom, please." I laughed. "What are you doing today?"

Closing his eyes and pulling me into him, he sighed. "Besides hiding from Cherish until her dinner tonight, nothing. What you got going on?"

"Don't do my friend like that. It's her birthday. We gotta treat her like the princess she is."

He smirked. "I already treat her like the spoiled brat she is. I can afford to take a break for a few hours before she break my pockets. Speaking of pockets, do you happen to know how me and Keem got stuck with the bill for this birthday dinner?"

Again, his eyes opened, but I quickly shut mine. "Nahhhh, you my woman now. You gotta tell Daddy all the secrets."

Slowly opening my eyes, I put my forehead against his and traced the edge of his jaw with my finger. "It don't matter how good you lay down that dickadryl as you call it; I'll never break girl code." Placing a kiss on his lips, I smiled and slipped out of the bed.

"I'ma let you slide today, but we'll circle back to the subject."

"Mmhmm. We gotta figure out what we're getting her."

"I'm getting her what she likes – money. If you wanna put your name on the card along with mine, that's cool with me, bae."

I stood at the edge of the bed with my arms crossed and my face scrunched up. "Boooo, tomato, tomato. That's whack, Wizdom."

Sitting up against the headboard, he chuckled. "She already on yo' head about her gift, huh?" he said knowingly.

I couldn't keep a straight face if I tried. Busting out laughing, I fell onto the bed. "Bae, she sent me and Ash a picture of a jet last night. Talkin' bout if we love her, we'll get it the ski mask way. What is wrong with your sister?"

Laughing, he pulled me up by my arms so that I was on top of him. "Cherish been a nutcase ever since we were kids. A spoiled nutcase."

"She's not spoiled." I tried to argue in her defense, knowing damn well she was. "She's just Cherish. My not so frugal best friend. And you know how much she loves feeling celebrated."

He raised an eyebrow at me, calling bullshit. "That's the elevated definition of spoiled, my baby. But she got it honest. My mama the same way. So, if my money and a card ain't up to your standards, what do you suggest?"

"What about jewelry? Something custom. She'd love that."

Reaching down and squeezing my booty, he gave it a light

smack. "I'm wit it. Whatever you think will keep my title as favorite sibling."

Before I could respond, my phone rang on my nightstand. Reaching over to grab it, the screen lit up with Cherish's name. "This don't make no sense." I laughed, holding the phone up for him to see the screen. Answering quickly, I rolled onto my back and got comfortable on his chest.

"**Happy birthday to one of the baddest bitches I know!**" I yelled out before she could speak.

"**You betta fuckin' know it!**" she exclaimed, her hyped energy spilling through the phone like she'd been waiting all night to hear the birthday wishes. "**Where's the birthday parade though? I half expected y'all to be at my door with a second line band.**"

"**Here she go,**" Wizdom mumbled, and I snickered.

"**That's Wiz?**" she inquired. "**Is that my favorite brother in the whole wide world?**"

"**Aye, you bogus as hell, dawg.**" I could hear her brother, Keem, in the background.

"**Hella bogus,**" Wiz cosigned with a chuckle just as a Face-Time request came through.

Connecting the video, Cherish's face appeared, bright eyed and bushy tailed. "**I figured y'all wanted to see my face. What y'all doing?**"

"**Fuck all that,**" Wiz let out. "**You told Keem he was your favorite?**"

"**Huh?**" Cherish played slow.

"**Nah, ain't no huh! Tell him how you got me out here playing chauffeur and been calling me yo' favorite.**"

"**It's my birthday, y'all. Don't do that to me. Don't make me choose.**" She dramatically threw her hand up to her forehead.

"**Bogus!**" Wizdom and Keem said at the same time, making me laugh.

"Anyway," I interjected, "**what time are we meeting up for brunch?**"

"**Brunch and shopping,**" she corrected. "**Meet up is at eleven. Which means you have a good two hours to get ready. I already spoke to Ashlynn.**" Leaning into the phone, she tried to whisper. "**She was over at Keem house this morning. He dropped her off and came to pick me up. You ain't hear that from me though.**"

"**Mannn, ion even wanna be yo' favorite no mo'. You out here tellin' a nigga business.**"

Cherish flipped the camera, and we could see Keem's face.

"**Nigga, you tellin' yo' own business. Over there smiling and shit.**" Wizdom called him out.

"**Mannn, I'ma put yo' ass out on the highway.**" He swatted the phone while Cherish laughed.

I grinned, thinking about how hush Ashlynn had been about her fake sneaking around with Keem. I couldn't wait to bring it up at brunch.

"**Alright, girl. Let me get up and start getting myself together. I'll see you in a few.**"

"**Okay, boo. Please don't be late. Oh, and Wiz, whatever money you send her with, go head and double it. Thank ya kindly.**"

Reaching over me, Wizdom ended the call.

"You so wrong." I laughed. "She gon' get you."

"I ain't thinkin' bout Cherish. She said you got two hours though. Since you'll be gone most of the day, come let Daddy suck on that pretty pink pearl. Put an extra pep in ya step."

Happy to oblige, I tossed my phone to the side and set myself up in the 69 position. Pulling the sheet from his body, I wrapped my hand around his dick while sitting on his face. "Remember, I can't be late, baby."

"She said for me to double the money. Suck that dick like you want your homegirl to have a happy birthday."

I walked into Angels of Harlem, thirty-five minutes past the scheduled meet up time, with my head held high. I knew Cherish was going to let me have it, but the couple rounds with Wizdom was worth the fight.

"Not you gliding in here with the Kool-Aid smile like you're not late on **my** birthday." Cherish called me out before I could even make it to the table.

"I know, I know. I'm sorry. You real cute, boo. I like this look." Spring had made its debut, and the sleeveless graphic tee went well with the maxi skirt and fitted cap she wore. Leaning over her chair, I kissed her cheek. "Where's Ash?"

"In the bathroom. Probably went to sneak and call Keem. Today is supposed to be about me. I would've called my other friends had I known y'all was gon' be so trifling today."

"Girl, shut up. You're so extra." Waving off her dramatics, I took a seat and picked up one of the mimosas that set on the table. "Here," I held my drink in the air, "cheers and be merry." She held her glass up begrudgingly and clinked it with mine. "Fix your face, beautiful."

"Unhn, unhn. Not you sounding like my brother."

I giggled and sipped my drink. Scanning the semi packed restaurant, I spotted Ashlynn making her way through the people.

"Wassup, Johnny come lately?" Kissing my cheek, she sat down across from me. "I'm glad you finally got here cause this chick was getting on my nerves."

Cherish gave her the finger and rolled her eyes. "Now that the gang's all here, we can really start the celebration." She held her drink up, and we followed. "Cheers to waking up a bad bitch once again, but this time, a year older. Although y'all both tried me this morning, I just know that my jet is on someone's tarmac, just waiting for me, with a big, red bow on it."

"I love that even at your big ass age, you still have a vivid imagination. Cheers to you, sista." Ashlynn clinked glasses with her, and we all laughed. She knew damn well she wasn't getting no damn jet.

After two rounds of mimosas and a round of French 75s, we found ourselves downtown, in and out of boutiques. Each boutique was glossier and more expensive than the last, right up Cherish's alley. And while I loved shopping just as much as the next woman, I didn't linger for long, especially when I was a little tipsy and stepping in platform heels.

"Alright, this the last store. I promise," Cherish announced, holding three bags in each hand.

"You damn right it is," Ashlynn confirmed. "My damn ankles hurting in these shoes."

"It's all that ass you carrying around." I playfully smacked her butt. "Y'all go in there. I'm gonna run in the sneaker store real quick. I wanna get my niece a pair of shoes."

"The baby is six months old, Lacey. How many shoes you gon' buy her?"

"You sound like Lance. I'ma get my girl as many as I feel like buying. She gon' know her aunty had money."

Since the day my niece had graced the world with her presence, I'd been spoiling her rotten. And I made sure to double down whenever my brother would tell me I was doing too much. At the rate I was going, Lance nor his fiancée would need to buy clothes or shoes until she reached the toddler stage. Entering a Champs sneaker store, I headed straight for the baby shoes. I busied myself with their limited selection for a few minutes before deciding on two pairs that I liked. Heading to the register with my purchase, my phone rang. Fishing it out of my purse, I smiled seeing the incoming call from Wizdom.

Connecting my AirPod, I answered. **"You must miss me already."**

"I do. Wanted to hear your voice. You enjoying yourself?"

"I am. We're out shopping. I'm in Champs getting Amaya some sneakers. And before you say it, I don't care. That's my..." The beeping sound indicating an incoming call cut me off. Checking the screen, there was an unknown number. **"Hold on, baby. I have a call coming in."** Clicking over, the call connected.

"Hello? Lacey?" Recognizing Quan's voice, I hit the end button so quick, I hung up on Wizdom.

Tucking my phone into my back pocket, my eyes darted around the store, thinking that Quan would appear at any moment. It had been months since I'd heard his voice, and there was no reason for him to reach out now.

"Miss, I said I'll take you here," the sales associate repeated with sharpness in her tone, waving me forward.

I blinked and nodded before walking up to the register. "Sorry bout that," I said, handing her the small shoe boxes.

She flashed a phony smile and rang up my purchase. "That will be $109.52."

Taking out my wallet to pay, my phone rang again, but this time, I didn't check the caller id nor bother to reach for it. While Wizdom may have been calling back, there was a possibility that it was Quan again. Either way, I needed a minute.

"Thank you," the sales associate said, holding my bag out for me.

Politely snatching it from her, I turned to leave the store and spotted the girls walking in.

"Y'all ready?" I asked, not noticing the irritation in my tone.

"What happened?" Ash questioned, picking up on it.

"And don't lie," Cherish added.

"Quan called."

"Ahh hell," Cherish let out, and I responded with a nod.

Ahh hell was right. If Quan was calling, I knew some bullshit was sure to follow.

2

———————

WIZDOM

*L*acey's pussy must've had that crack that hit back in the 80s in it cause she had me saying some strange shit. While I was sure I wanted kids, I didn't think we were at that stage of planning just yet. Granted, the unprotected sex was a set up for such conversation, but I still didn't believe it was something either of us wanted to discuss. The responsible thing would be to strap up, but I didn't see it happening unless she pushed the issue. Until then, the waterpark between her legs would be my personal playground.

Just thinking about her pussy made me pick up the phone to call her. Only before we could get into a full conversation, the call dropped. Figuring she was in a bad signal area, I decided not to call back and wait for her to call instead. I'd been chilling at her place since she left a few hours ago, and now it was time for me to get up and handle my business before the celebration later. Being at Lacey's crib always made a nigga a little lazy. It was peaceful, like her aura when she slept beside me.

Grabbing something to throw on from the space she insisted on giving me in her closet, I headed for the shower. Lacey made it clear that she wanted me to feel as comfortable as I made her when she was over at my crib. Since we'd locked in, she made sure to pull out the red-carpet treatment for me. She didn't half step, no matter how late or how early I came through. If I was hungry, she made sure I ate. If I needed to decompress, she gave me her ear to listen and her body when I needed release. Shit, if a nigga just needed to sit in silence, she was down for that too.

Steam filled the room as I stepped into the shower. The water hit my skin, relieving the tightness in my muscles. I needed to get my ass back to the gym. The only workout I'd been doing lately was limited to bussin' Lacey's ass up every time I got the chance to. My mind wandered – mostly to her but also to the rest of my day. I'd put in a call to my jeweler to get a necklace ordered for Cherish. With it being on such short notice, the best he could do was engrave the heart pendant on the necklace. So long as it was rocked out, I knew my spoiled brat would love it.

Fresh out the shower, I got dressed and checked my personal phone to see if Lacey had hit me back. She hadn't, but there were messages from my mom, Keem, and Suge. My mom's message was to confirm that I would still be meeting up with her and Keem to go over the last-minute stuff for Cherish's dinner. Keem's message was a complaint about him being designated chauffer for the day and how I should pick up the dinner tab on my own to even the playing field. I hit that nigga with a smooth hell no and went to Suge's message.

RightHand: What's the move today?

Me: I'm headed your way. Which house you at?

RightHand: Eastside. Hurry up. These niggas gettin' on my nerves, acting like they don't know what they supposed to be doing. Tryna take a nap before tonight.

Suge was my right hand and one of my greatest assets. She was family – not by blood but by bond and loyalty. She'd been my ace from the dirt, and we'd seen plenty ups in the game, had our fair share of downs, and somehow still came out on top. It wasn't common to see a man with a woman as his number two. Suge wasn't your average woman though. She carried herself like me and Keem.

A tomboy from the day I met her, she was harder than a lot of niggas I knew. Still, I was protective of her, even though I knew she was more than capable of handling herself. Sliding both of my phones into my pocket, along with my wallet, I put my jacket on and headed out the door. Taking the elevator down to the parking garage, I slid into my S-Class and made my way to the Eastside. Although Suge played the hood more than me, I'd been checking in more often the last few months, especially after having to shoot Slim's simple-minded ass. I hadn't had any issues out of him since then, still I made it my business to tap in consistently.

Pulling onto the street, my phone rang. Seeing the incoming call from Suge, I answered. **"I'm outside."**

"Cool. I'm coming out." A couple minutes later, I watched her walk out of the building, stopping to say a few words to the lookouts before bopping over to my car.

Dressed in a pair of Purple label jeans, Off White sneakers, and hoodie, Suge's attire screamed YN. I couldn't help but to comment on it when she got in on the passenger side.

"You know you look more and more like shorty every day, right?"

"I just got in the car, my nigga. Don't piss me off," she snapped.

"How you gon' be mad about a comparison that's getting you all the bitches?" I chuckled.

"Nigga, I get bitches off my swag alone, and I'm handsome, not because they think I look like Young M.A. And her dick don't do what my dick do. Trust me."

"How? They both rubber, Suge."

She threw a punch at me that I blocked and laughed. "Shut yo ass up."

"Aight. Aight. How shit lookin' out here?"

"The way it's supposed to. Workers in place, product moving, money stacking. Them niggas just act a lil' slow sometimes. Where you coming from?"

"Mindin' my business."

Suge raised an eyebrow. "Lacey?"

I smirked. "Here you go, in a nigga business."

"That tells me everything I need to know. I like her for you. Shit, kinda liked her for me. But if your sister quit playin', we can start doing double dates and shit." She said the shit so casually, it caught me off guard.

"Who sister?"

She leaned back in her seat. "Stop playin' wit me, dawg."

Chuckling, I shook my head. "I keep tellin' you Cherish don't swing that way."

"And I keep tellin' you it's only a matter of time. Anyway, what should I get her?"

"Shit," I shrugged, "hell if I know. I was gonna give her a card and a couple dollars. Lacey wasn't feeling that shit. Now, I'm down a good three racks on a necklace."

"Aight, bet. So, I gotta spend five. Lemme go give these niggas the rundown for the rest of the day, and I'll see you at dinner." She went to open the car door and stopped. "What's the attire again?"

"I ain't the party planner. I'm just paying for the venue and food."

"Three-piece suit it is." She got out the car, and I bust out laughing, just envisioning her in a suit.

"She bout to look just as stupid as Fallon did bringing them damn ballons to a party she wasn't invited to," I said out loud as I drove off.

I ENTERED THE NAIL SHOP WHERE MY MOTHER REQUESTED I MEET her and Keem. They were really working my boy today, and I knew he was pissed. He was always the easier of the two of us to convince to do something. Posted in the waiting area, he looked like he'd rather be anywhere else on the planet but here.

"How long y'all been here?" I asked, taking a seat beside him.

"Long enough for me to be irritated and to know that this is your mother and sister's last ask of me for the month. I'm so glad God didn't give a nigga a daughter cause this shit crazy."

"You be tryna be the favorite when all you gotta do is chill. You gotta remember Cherish got a man, and Mama..."

"Betta not have no man and I don't know about it," he cut me off.

"I was gonna say Mama don't be needing much. She just like our company. And you over here talkin' bout you happy you ain't got a daughter. You got a woman though."

"Who?" he questioned with a sly smile.

"You still pretending like you and Ash ain't a thing, huh?"

"Nah. I definitely fuck with her heavy, but I ain't putting a title on it until she's ready to have that conversation. She know what it is though. She know not to play wit a nigga feelings."

I felt him. After the failed relationship with his baby mother, who was once the love of his life, Keem vowed that he'd never put too much stake in another woman. That bitch took my brother through it. And in turn, he took us through it. We all but celebrated when he finally decided to step away. It was a good thing too. I knew ol' girl was tired of Cherish having to get on her ass every time Keem came around us with a complaint. He wasn't the least bit soft, but he had a different kind of heart when it came to women.

I could say it was the way we were raised. It was the very reason why I was soft when it came to Lacey to a certain extent. My mama raised us to take care of a woman's heart. And in doing so, it didn't mean we stopped being the alpha males she bred. It meant that we had to have balance in order to have a successful relationship. I thought Keem had fully grasped that concept now.

"Here she come now," I said, pointing to my mother, who made sure to say bye to everyone in the salon before finally making it over to us.

"Okay, I'm ready," she announced. "Wassup, son?" She greeted me with a hug and a pat on the back. Looking down at Keem, she smiled. "You ready to go, grumpy man?"

"Been ready. Did you pay the people?"

"Yep. I need to go to one…"

"Hell nah. No," he let out, shaking his head.

She laughed and looped her arms with both of ours. "I'm just playing. Which one of you taking me home?"

"That would be him." He pointed at me while we walked out of the salon. "I gotta make a couple moves."

"Nigga, stop lying. You ain't got shit goin' on." I called him out on his bogus excuse.

Giving me the finger, he kissed our mother's cheek and skated off to his car.

"I'ma give him a pass this time," she said. "I took up most of his day. I wanted to see you anyway."

"What I do?"

She smirked. "Nothing. I wanna talk about Lacey."

"What about her?"

"We'll talk in the car. Come on." Walking ahead of me, she went over to the driver's side.

"Ma, what you doing?" I laughed.

"I'ma drive. I need you focused for these questions. Unlock the door."

"I gotta pull up on my jeweler to get Cherish gift."

"Okay. Why you actin' like I don't know how to take directions? Unlock the car, boy."

Shaking my head, I hit the locks and got in on the passenger side. Moms was a straight shooter, so there was no telling what kind of questions she'd ask. The fact that she wanted to talk about Lacey, I knew the line of questioning was likely to be serious.

"Hop on the expressway and I'll guide you from there," I instructed.

"Nah, put the address in the GPS and it'll guide me. You need to focus on hearing me."

Rather than go back-and-forth with her, I typed the address into the navigation system, and she pulled off.

"So, wassup, Ma? You must've had one of your dreams or something."

"I did. And we'll get to that. How are things going with you and Alacea?"

"Good. That's my baby. But you know that, Ma. We talk about her every time I see you."

"I know. I really like her for you. I like the person you've been since being with her."

I looked over at her with my eyebrows furrowed and offense written all over my face. "What you tryna say, Ma? I'm the same person. I just have a woman now."

"Not like that, son. The you with her is different. You're not always on the go. I see you more. And not just in fleeting moments. Do you notice that we talk everyday now, Wizdom?

Prior to Lacey, we spoke a good twice a week, and I'd be lucky if I laid eyes on you three times in a month."

I thought about what she said and had to admit she was right. She could attribute my steady presence to Lacey. After losing her biological parents at a young age, Lacey stressed the importance of staying tapped in with her people daily and made sure I did the same.

"I can see that. I didn't know you felt a way about me not being around as much though. I always make sure I'm present when it counts, Ma. You know that."

Stopping at a red light, she glanced over at me. "I'm yo' mama, Wizdom. Every moment counts to me. And with the field you chose to work in, they count even more."

Nodding, I held my hand out for her to take. "I get it. You've been missing your favorite son. That's all you had to say, lady."

"Boy, go on." She laughed, slapping my hand away. "My only favorite is my grandson and the baby you have on the way will be added."

"There it go. So, that's what you had a dream about?"

"Yep. Saw your daughter clear as day. Turn here, right?"

I chuckled. "What the GPS say, Ma?"

"Don't make me cuss yo' ass out in the middle of our mother/son moment. Where I go, boy?"

"Get off on the exit and make a right. When you had the dream?"

"A couple weeks ago. That's why I mentioned you looking well rested. When I was pregnant with you, your dad slept more than me."

"Your dream may be a little bit off base this time, Ma. I told you what that girl be doing to me. Lacey ain't pregnant. I would know."

She whipped her head back in my direction. "And how the hell would you know, Wizdom? You got somebody pregnant before, and I don't know about it?"

"You know better than that. I'm just saying. She hasn't been moody, her appetite hasn't changed, her stomach ain't growing, the pu..."

"Wizdom!" She punched my arm.

"Aight." I laughed. "But yeah. You get what I'm saying."

"Pregnancy symptoms aren't one size fits all, son. Has she taken a test?"

I shook my head no. "Haven't seen a reason to."

"Well, now you have one," she stated matter-of-factly. Parking in front of the jewelry store, she turned off the ignition and got out. "Think and move, son. We don't have much time before this dinner."

Since a child, I'd never known any dream my mother had not to become a reality at some point in my life. At the same time, I felt there was no way Lacey was pregnant, and we both missed it. Putting the conversation aside, I made a mental note to mention it to Lacey in a few days. Shit, I needed a minute to process the possibility myself.

———

ONE ERRAND LED TO THREE, AND BEFORE I KNEW IT, THE SUN HAD dipped, and night had fallen. After dropping my mother off at home, I headed back to Lacey's place. We agreed that I would get dressed there, so we could leave together. She'd sent me a text once she made it back home, letting me know that she'd likely be asleep once I got back. Taking that into consideration, I entered quietly, locking the door behind me. Setting Cherish's gift down, I walked into the living room where Lacey was curled up on the couch, sound asleep.

A throw blanket partially covered her body, leaving one ass cheek exposed in her lace panties. I wanted to squeeze it, but by the way she slept with her mouth slightly agape, I could tell she was tired. She looked peaceful. Serene. Quite the opposite of the porn star she was when she rode my dick the night before. Taking in her skin, her lips, her cheeks, and even her thighs, I searched for any signs of pregnancy, as if I really knew what the hell to look for. Thinking she'd feel me staring at her and stir awake, I gently pulled the blanket to fully cover her body. As I turned to leave the room, her phone vibrated violently on the coffee table.

Reaching down to silence it, I caught the caller id. It read unknown number. No sooner than I hit the button to silence the vibration, a text came through from an unsaved number. The message simply read:

It's Quan.

My jaw clenched, and a scowl spread across my face. *Fuck is this nigga doing contacting my woman?* I thought to myself. I stared at the phone for a few seconds, waiting to see if it would vibrate again.

"Hey, baby," she greeted, opening her eyes and stretching. "You just got here?"

"Yeah," I replied dryly.

"You okay?" she questioned, her eyes full of concern as she sat up, removing the blanket from her body.

"Yeah. I'm bout to hop in the shower and get ready for tonight."

"Okay. We can take one together." Standing from the couch, she walked to me and wrapped her arms around my neck. "Did you get a gift that would represent us well?"

"Yep. It's in the bag in the kitchen."

"Good job, baby. Kiss me." I leaned down and kissed her lips twice. "You sure you okay?"

"I'm sure. Come on, let's shower."

"Okay. Let me grab my phone to text Ashlynn real quick."

"Text her after, bae. We on a tight schedule."

"You're right. And knowing you, we won't just be washing up." Winking, she grabbed my hand and led me to the bedroom.

I felt it best to stir her away from her phone for the moment. I didn't know how she'd explain her ex reaching out or if she even felt she should. Some things were better left alone. The last thing I wanted was to have tension looming over us on my sister's celebratory night. It would be addressed at a better time and place though. There was no way around that.

3

ALACEA

After a round of back shots in the shower and a two-hour nap, we were dressed and riding out to the restaurant. At Cherish's request, we wore all black and looked good as a unit. I'd chosen a corset waist, strapless, bandage dress that held every curve I possessed hostage. On my feet were a pair of YSL heels that added another inch to my height, making it so that I was at Wizdom's shoulder. By the way he stole glances at me and kept one hand on my thigh while the other manned the steering wheel, I knew he approved of my choice of attire. But while I could feel him physically, mentally he seemed to be elsewhere.

Music played, but we had barely said more than a few words to each other since leaving my house. In the back of my mind, I knew why, but I refused to be the one to bring those thoughts to the surface. As we'd prepared to leave my place, I'd grabbed my phone from the living room, and there, on the screen, was a message from Quan. I didn't recognize the number, but there it was, on my notification screen. Out of all the opportunities this man had to be persistent, he chose now – when I was in a relationship, being treated like a queen, getting finer, and thriving. Just like a nigga to realize what he had after it was gone.

"I'm glad we got that nap in. I'm sure Cherish is gonna have us out most of the night," I said, breaking the silence.

"You know she's gonna get her money's worth."

I chuckled. "Yeah. When you're ready to head out, you just say the word."

Silence lingered in the air before he spoke again. "Quan texted you."

I looked over at him, half expecting him to move his hand from my thigh. He didn't. Instead, he gently rubbed it. I took it as his way of letting me know that it was okay to be honest about the text. So, I did.

"Yeah. I saw it," I admitted. For a second, I almost went too far and told him about the call I received earlier.

"Any reason why he would be texting you out the blue?"

"No. It caught me by surprise too."

"Aight," he replied dully.

"Are you mad?" I asked, placing my hand atop of his.

"You got something you need to say to that man or something you need to hear him say?" Pulling up to the restaurant, he parked and turned to me.

"No," I replied, my answer more delayed than I intended, making me sound guilty as hell.

He cocked his head to the side and squinted his eyes. "I wanna be clear when I say this, beautiful. I fuck witchu heavy. I have plans for us but understand that I'm not going for **nothing** strange. If you need some kind of closure from that situation, get that. All I ask is that you be upfront about it. Am I gonna like it? Fuck no. But I can respect the fact that there may be a part of you that feels healing still needs to be done. You don't have to give me an answer tonight. But I expect one at some point. For now, let's go inside and enjoy ourselves."

Sitting across from him, I didn't know how to respond. I was healed from all the bullshit I went through with Quan, but would closure be nice? Yes. Did I feel like that nigga owed me a few apologies? Hell yes. And if I was honest with myself, I wanted to know the why. It may sound futile to some, but after giving someone two years of my life that I couldn't get back, I felt like I deserved to know.

At the same time, my new man deserved more than that. I couldn't see myself disrespecting Wizdom. So, I said what was right.

"I don't need anything from him, bae."

Nodding, he got out of the car and walked over to my side to let me out. Placing my hand in his, I walked beside him, hoping that the conversation didn't make the dinner awkward. So far, we were off to a rocky start.

THE SPOT CHERISH BOOKED TO HOST HER DINNER WAS IN Midtown. Black and gold awnings framed the entrance, and the black carpet with white rose petals that Cherish had requested was a nice touch. I was skeptical about her being able to pull it off, but money talked. DonCelli's looked like money, and the smell of butter and wine hit your nose upon entry. It wasn't the kind of place you just walked into – you arrived. My girl stamped her arrival by this small touch alone.

"Aight, they got this rose petal shit right. I hope to see the same when we go inside. She betta be able to meet the owner for the tab they hit us with yesterday," Wizdom let out, holding the door open for me.

"Welcome to DonCelli's. Do you have a reservation?" the host asked with a welcoming smile.

"Yes. We're here with the party for Cherish McCombs," Wizdom answered.

"Oh, yes. Right this way."

We were led to a private dining area downstairs that glowed upon entry. The crystal pendant lights that hung from the ceiling cast a gold glow over the room that was absolutely beautiful. The black and gold décor went perfect with her theme, and everyone had gotten the memo that it was an all-black affair. The restaurant staff had outdone themselves, making the space intimate with candles spread throughout the room. The vibe was grown and sexy. It was easy to see why Cherish decided to have a no kids allowed gathering.

I'd come to know Wizdom's immediate family pretty well over the last few months we'd been together, so I was able to pull away from him to give a few hugs and kisses. I found Ashlynn near the back, seated comfortably next to Keem. Making my way over to her, I gave Keem a half hug while he stood to talk to Wizdom, who was a couple feet behind me.

"Hey, why you come in here fake smiling?" Ashlynn questioned before I could slide into the seat next to her.

"Damn, am I that obvious?" Straightening my shoulders, I adjusted my corset in an attempt to distract her from my face.

"Maybe not to everyone else, but to the person who's known you your whole life," she raised her hand, "it's pretty obvious."

"Alright, y'all, my baby bout to make her way inside," Ms. Angela announced.

"I'll tell you about it later," I said to Ashlynn while standing with my phone out to capture Cherish's entry.

Kash Doll's *Kash Kommandments* played through the surround sound system as she made her way through the doors of the private room. Stopping at the bottom step, she rapped the first verse of the song like she was straight out of the 313. Me and Ash hyped her up, singing along. There was no question as to who her best friends were. We made that known.

"Yeah, sis!" I encouraged, moving around so that I was able to capture her at every angle.

Once the music stopped, everyone yelled out happy birthday, drowning her in love. Making her rounds, she finally made it over to us.

"This ain't even the dress we seen on FaceTime. I like this one better, boo," Ashlynn complimented.

"Girlll, you don't even wanna know the drama behind the change. I…" Cherish was cut off by Suge's hand around her waist. I hadn't even seen her come in.

Ashlynn and I stood back, watching their whispered exchange.

"Wassup, y'all?" Suge finally acknowledged our presence.

"Heyy," we said in unison.

"Enjoy the party, Ma. I'll be around if you need me."

As soon as Suge swaggered off, we were on Cherish's head. "I'll be around if you need me, huh? Ummm, since when?"

"Yeah, Ma," Ashlynn egged on. "Since when you and Young M.A become a thing? And where's Keyon?"

"Party now. Answers to your questions tomorrow. Deal?" Cherish offered her hand for us to shake on her deal.

Seeing as she and Keyon were usually each other's shadow, I figured whatever she had to tell us could possibly ruin her mood. I wanted my girl to enjoy her night, so I agreed, shaking her hand.

"Ash!" I snapped, playfully nudging her.

She had her hands at her side and a straight face. "What? I'm only agreeing if you agree to tell us what's wrong with you too."

I shot her an incredulous look. "Now, what my business gotta do with this?"

"I don't know," Cherish interrupted, "but I'm the birthday girl and what I say goes. Now, shake my hand, dammit."

I snickered, and we sealed the deal with a three-way hand-shake before taking our seats. As the night progressed, the drinks flowed, and the waiters served endless appetizers before we got to the main course. I chose roasted chicken with garlic mashed potatoes and broccolini. I had Wiz get the fish because I had a taste for both dishes. When the waitress brought out his Chilean sea bass with wild rice and spinach, I second guessed my entrée. Like a good man, he fed me most of his while I only dibbled and dabbled in my plate.

"It's good?" He laughed, feeding me another piece of fish.

"So good," I replied, covering my mouth as I chewed. "That was my last bite though. Eat your food, baby."

Glancing down at his plate and then back at me, he smirked. "You ate half the fish, beautiful."

"I'm sorryyy," I dragged, pouting. "You want me to order you another one? I'ma order you another one." I put my hand up to flag the waitress over, and he pulled it back down.

"I'm good, baby. I didn't have much of an appetite anyway. So long as you cool, I'm straight."

"You sure? I can get you one to go. I'll even pay."

Smirking, he tilted his head down and kissed my lips. "I'm sure, big money."

"Mmmm. More please." I puckered my lips, and he kissed me twice.

"Alrightt with all that PDA," Suge said from across the table.

"Shut up." Wizdom tossed one of the napkins her way. "Let me go to the bathroom real quick, bae." As he stood, my phone vibrated in my purse.

"Okay." Pulling his arm from around me, he got up and walked off.

Checking my phone, I sighed deeply at the text notification displayed on my screen.

917-734-4627: Not sure if you got my other message but hit me when you can. It's important. Quan.

I rolled my eyes hard at him ending the message with his name like it was some kind of calling card. I wanted to respond to the message and warn him not to reach out again, but any response to Quan, whether good or bad, would indicate an open line of communication. Instead, I blocked the number and placed my phone down on the table. I had every intention on finishing my food until I got that text.

Wizdom returned to the table, reclaiming his seat next to me. "You good?"

"Yes, baby. I'm fine." I forced my facial expression to match my words.

"You wanna give ya girl her gift?" He held up a bag that was neatly tied with a white bow, concealing Cherish's necklace.

"No. You give it to her. I wanna see her reaction."

Cherish sat two seats down from us on the other side of the table.

"Aye," Wizdom called out to Suge, who was texting on her phone. "Pass this down to the birthday girl."

Suge took the bag and went to peek inside.

"Gimme my stuff, Suge!" Cherish yelled out.

"Baby, that's so ghetto. You could've gone down there and handed it to her." I laughed.

"That nigga ain't slick, Lacey. He just want it to be known that he got her something expensive," Keem noted.

Wizdom laughed, brushing him off.

"I hope it's good, bro," Cherish said, reaching inside the bag and pulling out the velvet jewelry box. Her hand went to her mouth, muffling a scream when she opened the box, revealing the white diamonds. "Wizdom!" she shrieked. Jumping up from her chair, she skipped over to us and threw her arms around his neck.

"Custom," he bragged casually. "Happy birthday, Bam Bam. Say thank you to my baby too. It was her idea."

"Awww," she cooed, moving over to me to give me the same love. "This is so dope. I love y'all."

"Only the best for our spoiled princess," I teased.

Sticking her tongue out, she turned her attention to Keem.

"Aight now, Keem. Let me see how you coming." Any chance she got, Cherish made sure to egg on the favorite sibling competition.

Keem pulled out his phone and handed it to Ashlynn with a head nod. "Bae, call the man and tell him to land the jet at LaGuardia airport. Wizdom got me fucked up."

I bust out laughing along with the rest of the table as we watched her unlock his phone, pretending to dial a number with a straight face.

"Tell 'em to park it next to the one I got her," Suge added, sending a wink Cherish's way.

Giggling, Cherish walked back around to her seat, making sure to brush her hand across the back of Suge's neck on the way there. My eyes found Ashlynn's, who smirked, letting me know she had peeped the familiar gesture as well.

"You wanna get a to go box for the rest of your food?" Wiz asked.

"Yes, pl…" A wave of nausea came over me, causing my hand to shoot up to my mouth in an effort to hold back what I felt coming up. "Bathroom," I mumbled to avoid potentially ruining dinner.

He got the hint, hopping up and escorting me to the bathroom. "You need me to come inside?"

I wildly shook my head no, using my free hand to push open the door to the ladies' room and rushing to the last stall. I couldn't get the seat up fast enough before I threw up both his meal and mine.

"We got it, Wizdom," I heard Cherish say. "You can't go in the ladies' bathroom, crazy."

I could hear him fussing at her, and then Ashlynn called out my name.

"Where you at, Lace?"

"Last stall," I managed to verbalize just as another wave of nausea hit me, sending me hurling over the toilet.

"We right here, boo," Cherish assured lovingly.

Standing upright, I leaned against the door to compose myself. "I need something to rinse my mouth out. There's a small bottle of Scope in my bag. Can someone bring me a bottle of water too?"

I overheard Ashlynn delegating the task to Wizdom, but he didn't budge.

"I got it. I need her to tell me she good before I go anywhere though." His tone was assertive, letting Ash know that he was serious.

Flushing the toilet, I peeked out of the stall for him to hear me. "I'm good now, baby. I just need the water and mouthwash."

"See?" Ashlynn playfully taunted. "Go get the stuff, man."

He returned seconds later with the items, only for the girls to shoo him away once again.

"One thing a bitch gon' do is try to outshine the birthday girl," Cherish joked, handing me a couple wet paper towels.

"Girl, go ta hell." I snatched them from her. "I feel so disgusting. Damn."

"You know I'm just fuckin' witchu. Seriously though, what's wrong?"

"I don't even know. Nothing seemed off about the food I ate. I was fine on the way here." Taking the mouthwash and water from Ash, I rinsed my mouth twice.

"I hope it wasn't the food. I already know Wizdom out there inspecting everything on your plate and likely about to find his way in them people kitchen to speak to the chef personally."

"Girl, he would not do that."

Cherish put her hand on her hip and cocked her head to the side. "You ain't gotta be around Wiz that long to know that nigga is 730. He in that kitchen."

"Ion know." Ashlynn shrugged. "I don't know Wizdom that well, but in getting to know Keem and knowing this chick right here," she nodded toward Cherish, "bat shit crazy."

"And we wear it proudly," Cherish said with her head held high. "Something gotta be wrong with you, Lacey."

Ash squinted her eyes, watching me closely. "Ho, is you pregnant?"

"Ashlynn, please. Ain't nobody pregnant. I don't know what's wrong with my stomach."

"Okay, then. Can we talk about what was wrong with your face earlier?"

"No. We need to get back out there, so Cherish can finish her dinner. I've had enough attention on me tonight. Right, Cherish?" I glanced at her, gesturing my head toward the bathroom exit.

"You might as well spill the tea," Cherish pushed.

Sucking my teeth, I trashed the water and tightened the top on the mouthwash. Swiping my hand over the sink, I fake admired the marble in an attempt to stall.

"Listen, I'm already sharing my birthday spotlight with you, Lace. Don't piss me off. Spill."

"Quan texted me before we got here. Wizdom saw the text before I did and mentioned it to me. He asked if I needed some kind of closure. Well, it wasn't so much of an ask as it was an implication that I may need closure – if that makes sense."

Ash rolled her eyes. "That explains your whole demeanor when you came in. I thought you already blocked his knock off Trey Songz lookin' ass."

"I did. I blocked the two numbers I had. I didn't know this one."

"I hope you didn't tell Wizdom he called you earlier. You know how you get to being too honest and shit," Cherish let out.

"Hell no," I replied with wide eyes. "It's bad enough that he saw the text. I mean, we're doing so good. And y'all know how I feel about Wiz. That's my boo, and I don't want Quan's sudden reappearance to shake up what we're working to build. Which is why I blocked him when he texted me again."

"Again?" Cherish and Ash said in unison.

"I let you slide on the first text cause you can't avoid what you don't know but not blocking him the first time got me side eyeing you."

I wasn't the least bit surprised about Ashlynn being so vocal.

"No, forreal," Cherish added. "You losing me."

"Well, it's done now. However, I still feel uneasy." My head dropped, and they both took their place at the left and right of me.

"Don't trip, cousin," Ashlynn offered. "You know when them old niggas get even a thought in their head that their good thing is off living their happily ever after without them, they activate their inner bitch ass nigga. You see the type of time Tim be on. Just pressed and silly looking. Put Quan out of your mind and stay focused on who's in front of you – Wizdom."

"Yeah, cause you fuckin' wit' a big dog now." Cherish flexed. "I know it. I've been around him my whole life. And he ain't gon' play about nothing he love."

I smiled at the four-letter word that could either make or break a relationship. I'd developed those kind of feelings over the last few months but had yet to express them to Wizdom – mainly out of fear that he may not be in that space yet. I'd made the mistake of telling Quan I loved him too early and found myself giving more than I ever could get back.

"I hear y'all, and I'm focused. Trust me. The last thing I want Wizdom to think is that he made a mistake by taking a chance on us."

"Cool. Now that your crisis is no longer a crisis, can we get back to the reason we're gathered here this evening?" Cherish pointed to herself.

"Yes, we can, boo. Thank y'all for coming to my aid."

"Always, sista. Back to the celebration we go."

"Like nothing happened," Ashlynn adlibbed as we left the bathroom to rejoin the party.

Only pretending like nothing happened would be easier for them than me. I'd told them about Quan, but what I hadn't mentioned was that this wasn't the first time I'd thrown up this week. In fact, I'd been having these vomiting spells the last two weeks. I'd been able to hide it from Wizdom when he was around so far, but tonight may have just opened the door to my cover being blown. I had yet to take a test – too scared to take one. The lingering nauseating feeling wasn't just physical – it was tied to something deeper.

Still, I thugged it out the rest of the dinner, although it was a blur of laughter, side jokes, and camera flashes from the photographer Cherish had hired for the night. I was there physically, but mentally, I was home. I played my part, leaning into Wizdom, giving reassuring smiles each time he asked if I was okay. As dinner came to a close, Cherish stood from her seat.

"Thank y'all from the bottom of my heart for showing up and showing out tonight," she expressed, teary eyed. "I don't know if it's because y'all didn't wanna hear my mouth if y'all left me hanging or because y'all love me so much..."

"I'll take the first reason for 500, Alex," Keem interrupted with his hand up.

"Shut up, Keem." She laughed. "Whatever the reason, know that I love and appreciate all of y'all for making this birthday a special one. Now, let's clear these people establishment, so we can really go turn up."

It was eleven o' clock, still early enough to party, but by the look on Wizdom's face, I knew my man was ready to head home. And I must say I was on the same type of time.

"Let me say goodnight to my people, then we can head out."

"Okay, baby. I'm gonna do the same." I went around the table, giving hugs, and when I reached Ms. Angela, she stood from the table.

"We still on for brunch this week, right?" she confirmed.

"Wouldn't miss it. I can't wait for you to meet my mom."

"Same, baby. We have a lot to discuss. Y'all drive safe. You're carrying precious cargo." We embraced, and when she pulled away, she rubbed my belly discreetly. Flashing a knowing smile, she walked off.

Precious cargo? I thought to myself. Did she know something I had yet to find out?

4

WIZDOM

The ride back to Lacey's place was quiet, mainly because she'd fallen asleep five minutes into the drive. Her head rested against the window with her hand cupped under her chin to hold it up. I thought about turning on some music to drown out my thoughts as I drove but decided against it. I actually needed the silence to sort out my thoughts from tonight.

Cherish's dinner was cool. Everything went smooth and according to plan. The owner had even offered to comp half of the tab after Lacey threw up. Now, that was the kind of customer service a nigga could fuck with. Moms swore up and down that her nausea had nothing to do with the food and everything to do with this baby I'd yet to mention to Lacey. I had mixed feelings. Something in my gut told me that our brief conversation about her ex still lingered in her mind.

It may have had something to do with how I approached the situation. I wasn't condescending. I didn't force her to speak on it nor was I accusatory in my tone when I brought the subject up. In other words, I wasn't a ho about it. Instead, I was upfront, which gave her the space to be honest with me. I would've picked up on it had she lied anyway. And while she didn't lie, something did shift in her the second I mentioned Quan and the text, however not in a way that made me think that the feelings were still there.

She tried to play it cool, but I was sure it took her by surprise when I brought up the idea of closure. Hence her delayed response. I didn't push the issue. It wasn't the time to. Still, I wanted my words to sink in because I meant everything I said. I tabled our talk to circle back to. I always filed anything I felt needed or was deserving of another conversation.

The thing was that I could give a fuck about Quan. What I cared about was the relationship that Lacey and I were building. His physical presence didn't threaten that. I could get a nigga gone in sixty seconds, no movie script. But I wasn't naïve. It was likely that what she went through in that relationship still rented a small space in her head.

They had history. And history had a funny way of presenting itself even when the person it was tied to didn't speak a word. I was open to her getting her closure – in a way that suited me of course. My only request was that she was honest. Shit, to keep it all the way real, she didn't have a choice but to keep it a hunnit with me. It was non-negotiable. Turning onto her block, I pulled into the parking garage and parked next to her truck. Shutting off the engine, I stirred her awake.

"We're here," I announced.

Sitting up straight, she looked to her left then her right – as if she were in a foreign place. "That was quick. Sorry for falling asleep on you, bae."

"You good, baby. Seems like you needed it. How you feeling?"

She paused before replying. "Better than I did at the restaurant."

I watched her carefully. "Yeah, about that…"

Her face tightened, giving way to a cautious stare.

"You threw up."

"I did. That was so embarrassing. I almost threw up on you, but you got the memo quick." She giggled softly.

"It was hard not to, beautiful. Was it the food?"

Again, she hesitated. "No. I don't think so." Reaching for my hand that rested on her thigh, she traced the outline of my fingers, avoiding my eyes.

"You wanna talk about the other possibilities?"

Glancing up at me, she exhaled. "We can."

Seeing as the door was open, I decided to present my mom's theory first. "When's the last time you had your dot?" I asked, mindful of my tone.

Our eyes locked, neither of us blinking as if we'd realized that her silence meant something.

"I'd have to check my app." She paused a few seconds before speaking again. "But it's not the first time I've thrown up."

"Today?" I quizzed.

"This week."

Her admission silenced me. I thought about the validity of my mother's dream and without responding, started up the car.

"Wait. Where we going?"

"To get a test, beautiful." Putting the car in reverse, I checked the cameras as I backed out of the spot.

"Bae, wait." She stopped me with her hand on my arm. "We can get one tomorrow."

"Tomorrow?"

"Yes."

Shifting gears, I pulled back into the spot. Reaching for my hand again, she laced our fingers together.

"I need a minute to digest the possibility. I don't wanna make it a thing just yet."

I nodded, taking in her feelings. "You scared?"

She let out an audible sigh. "Not scared. More nervous than

anything. I mean, this is a reason to be nervous. You not nervous? Am I trippin'?"

The way her facial expression changed with each question she posed made me laugh. "Which question you want me to answer first, baby?"

Her lips parted into a lazy smile. "All of 'em, smart ass."

"No to all," I replied, gently squeezing her hand. "I respect your decision to wait though. Can we agree not to wait past tomorrow?"

"Yes. Let's kiss on it."

Grabbing the back of her head, I gave her two pecks on her lips. "You wanna suck on it?" I smirked when she nodded.

"Can you lick on it?" she countered.

Biting my bottom lip, I nodded. "You gon' ride on it?"

"Reverse cowgirl." The thought of her feet planted on the bed, riding me with no hands, made my dick jump. Pressing her lips against mine again, she put her hand in my lap, rubbing my dick through the pants. "I can do the sucking now."

"Daddy's little freak." Reclining my seat, I gave her space to unbuckle my belt and free **her** dick.

Lacey's hands were soft. The rings she wore on her fingers gleamed under the dim light in the parking garage. And it was something sexy as fuck about seeing her hand wrapped around my dick with a fresh set of acrylic nails. I bricked up instantly at her touch.

"Feed him to me, baby," she whispered seductively. Spit dripped from her lips onto the tip of my dick before she opened her mouth wide.

Placing my hand on the back of her head, I thrust my hips upward slowly, taking my time feeding her. "More?"

She bobbed her head in response, making me bite my lip and grunt. We were only a couple seconds in before we caught a rhythm that was comfortable for her and pleasing to me. To the outside world, Lacey had this innocence she carried along with her confidence. It was the thing that made people gravitate to her. All that innocent and reserved shit went out the window behind closed doors. My baby gave up all her holes willingly.

GAWK. "Mmmm." *GAWK, GAWK.* "Sssss, mmmm."

Every time she let my dick hit the back of her throat, she made sure to lock eyes with me, adding a little more spit each time. The nastier she got, the more I was willing to give up.

"Suck that dick, beautiful. Damn."

Tilting my head to the side, I watched her through hooded eyes. Lacey was so fucking pretty. Her mouth was wet with spit bubbles in the corners, showing just how dedicated she was to giving me the sloppiest top ever.

"Shit. Stick ya tongue out, baby. I'ma bout to nut so hard on that pretty ass tongue."

"Sssss," she hissed. "Lemme have it, Dada."

That shit sent me over the edge, and before she could get her tongue out good, cum shot out my dick onto her lips and cheek. "Ahhh, ahhh."

"That's a first." She giggled, reaching into the glove compartment for the wipes I kept in the car for her.

"My bad, baby."

"You good," she replied, wiping her face then wiping and tucking my dick away casually. "Ready to go inside?"

"Yeah. But before we do, I wanna let you know that whatever the outcome of the test is, it's me and you, aight?"

"I appreciate the reassurance."

Pulling my seat back up, I kissed her forehead. "I got you."

One thing Lacey and I had in common was the fact that we were homebodies. Although she went out with my sister and her cousin sometimes, for the most part, she was cool playing the crib. I couldn't fuck with a chick that was a busybody if she wasn't handling some type of business. I didn't want her confined to the house either. There was always a happy medium, and she fell right into it.

"I'm gonna go take a shower. Can you put my food away for me?" she asked as we entered the house.

"Yeah." Taking the bag from her, I went to the kitchen, while she went in the opposite direction.

Placing the food in the fridge, I took out my phone to call Keem. I'd given him what I thought should cover my half of the tab for dinner and wanted to make sure that the owner had kept his word.

"**What's good?**" he answered on the second ring.

"**Where you at?**"

"**In the car. On my way to pick up Dooty. Wassup?**"

"**I thought y'all was going to the club.**" Glancing down at my watch, the time read a little after midnight. "**And why you picking him up so late? It's almost 12:30 in the morning.**"

"**And? My boy called me and asked me to pick him up. His mama probably gettin' on his nerves and shit. You know she can be irritating as fuck. I ended up dropping Ashlynn off with Cherish.**"

I laughed. "**Keem, how do you irritate a five-year-old, bruh?**"

"**Shiiiddd, Pooh ass can irritate an infant forreal. She just irritating. She be stressin' my lil' man. I gotta go rescue him.**"

For my nephew to only be five, he always had some shit going on. Dooty was smart as hell, and he knew how to stir up some shit. I knew as soon as Keem showed up at his baby mother's door at this hour, she was gonna be pissed. And knowing him, he wouldn't give a fuck. Keem didn't fuss or argue with Pooh. When it came to their son, he pretty much did what suited him and Dooty. Shit was wild.

"**Dooty hell, man.**"

"**He know it. Wassup tho?**"

"**I was just calling to make sure you didn't have any issues with the tab at the restaurant. They comped half, right?**"

"Yeah, they did. But you owe me $2.68. Yo' calculations was off, bruh."

"Mannn, I wish I would come out my pocket for two funky ass dollars."

"And sixty-eight cents, nigga. Don't try to shortchange me."

"Clear my line, man. I gotta call my mama."

"Oh, speaking of Mama. She said you bout to join fatherhood. Congrats, nigga. I knew yo' time would come."

"Ya mama need to stop tellin' my business." I caught myself grinning at the thought of being a dad. "We ain't take a test yet, so I can't say for sure."

"If Mama had a dream, then it's for sure. I'll put the bread up behind that. Remember she had that dream that I was gonna have a baby mama that I was gon' co-parent with but wouldn't really like? And boom, Pooh."

"Mannn, fuck outta here." I chuckled.

"Real shit. *Long Island Medium* ain't got shit on Ms. Angela. Ohhh, one more thing. We need to meet up and talk to Cherish ass at some point. How she gon' go gay on us and not say shit? I want Suge present too with they sneaky asses."

"Cherish ain't gay, Keem."

Lacey walked into the kitchen and stood at the counter across from me. She'd traded her dress for a silk robe. Her face was bare, and she had her hair up in her signature bun on top of her head.

"The hell she is. That nigga, Keyon, wasn't there tonight, and I know you peeped that shit with Suge. Or maybe you didn't. You was too busy in ya baby mama face."

"Aight, man. We'll talk."

"You damn right we will. I'll hit yo' line later. Love you, nigga."

"Love you too, bruh." The call disconnected, and I set my phone down.

"You up for watching a movie? I can set us up in the living room while you shower."

"Yeah. We can do that. You look refreshed." I walked up to her and wrapped my arms around her waist.

"A shower will do that to you. Go take yours so you can feel the same."

"Aight, what you got on under here though?" I asked, taking a peek inside her robe.

A sneaky grin graced her face. "Nothing. You still gotta eat to seal our deal. I wanted you to have easy access." Pulling me down by my neck, she kissed my ear. "Go shower so I can feed you," she whispered, licking my earlobe.

Rocked up again, I nodded. "Gimme twenty minutes."

"Okay. Let me set up." Pushing me back, she skipped off into the living room.

Ready to wine down for the night, I went to pick up my phone just as it buzzed on the counter. I expected it to be a message from Keem, letting me know that Pooh had, in fact, cussed him out when he got to her crib like I knew she would. Instead, it was a message similar to the one Lacey had received from Quan, only it was from Fallon.

Fallon: You crossed my mind the other day. I took it as a sign to reach out. How are you? Missing me yet?

"Fuck is this? Return of the exes?" I said out loud.

"You good, bae?" Lacey asked.

"Yeah. I'm straight." Selecting Fallon's contact, I went into the settings to block and delete her number. I wasn't about to fumble because she got nostalgic when a nigga crossed her mind. She had a solid nigga fucked up.

Satisfied that the deed was done, I made my way to the shower, only to be halted by my vibrating phone again. This time, it was an incoming call from Suge.

"**What happened?**" I asked as I picked up. If she was calling on the personal line and not the trap phone, it had to be big.

"**Somebody had their hands in the cookie jar. Need you to pull up on me.**"

"**Which kitchen?**"

"**New spot.**"

"**An hour.**"

"**Bet.**"

So much for a nightcap. Duty called, and as the boss, I had to answer.

5

———

ALACEA

$\mathcal{W}$ith our movie night paused due to Wizdom being called away to take care of business, I decided to catch up on a few episodes of *911* that I'd missed. However, it wasn't long before the TV was watching me due to me falling asleep in the first thirty minutes of the episode. I was on my third dream when the loud ringing of my phone jolted me up out of my sleep. It was an incoming call from the Emergency Service line. I'd added a special ambulance ringtone to distinguish from a personal call.

Clearing my throat, I reached for the phone on the coffee table to answer. **"Hello."**

"Lacey, it's Pri. I need you at the house, babe."

Moving the phone from my ear to check the time, the screen read 3:16 a.m. I sucked my teeth and put the call on speaker. **"How bad, Pri?"**

"Bad enough for me to need you and not them people. One to the shoulder. We did what we could, but we need a trained eye."

"Alright. I got you. Is the person conscious?"

"Yes."

"Okay. I'll see you in a minute. Keep pressure on the wound as best you can."

"Will do."

Usually, service went through Lance, but a select few people were able to contact me directly. Pri was one of them. She ran an afterhours gambling spot that the night owls often flocked to after the club. Everyone in Harlem knew Pri. She was the pretty gangsta who didn't take no shit. She employed an all-male staff at the gambling house that didn't play about her.

Though there were rules at Pri's House, it wasn't exempt from its fair share of drama. And when it got serious and someone got hurt, she called me. Getting up, I sent a text to Blind, letting him know I needed him to ride with me. I could've rode alone, seeing as the place was familiar, but I felt more comfortable having Blind with me. He was also a night owl, so I knew he'd be up and alert.

> Blind: You gon' have to come get me from Tati crib. My truck ain't got no gas in it. Plus, she done fucked a nigga so good, I don't think I can drive.

I shook my head as I replied.

> Me: First off, you irresponsible as hell for not having no gas in yo car. Second, you really irk my nerves. I didn't need to know all that. I'll be to you in thirty minutes. Meet me downstairs, ugly.

I was glad his destination was close to me and not far from where we had to go. Quickly dressing in my scrubs and a pair of New Balance Wiz had bought me, I grabbed my wallet and tossed it into my med bag. On my way out, I dialed Wizdom's number, and the call went straight to voicemail as expected. I followed up with a text to let him know where I'd be and not to worry because Blind would be with me. This would be my first late night call since we'd been together.

It was something he'd expressed that he didn't too much care for in the beginning. At the same time, he understood that it came with the territory. I loved my job, and I didn't plan on slowing down anytime soon. Unless, of course, we were expecting the unexpected. A baby would surely change the way I went about things.

While en route to Blind, he called.

"Yeah?"

"I'm ready. Where we going?"

"Pri's. I'm fourteen minutes out."

I could hear him suck his teeth before responding. **"You might as well turn back around, cuzzo. I ain't going nowhere near Pri's crazy ass."**

"Brandon," I called him by his government name, squinting my eyes as if he could see me, **"you did exactly what I told you not to do, didn't you?"**

"If your question is did I fuck Pri after you warned me not to, the answer is yes. But hear me out though."

"No. Hell no! I told you not to go down that road, and if you did, I ain't wanna hear nothing about it from either of you. And yo' ass coming with me. I don't care what you talkin' bout."

I could always count on Blind to do the exact opposite of what made sense. I knew him messing around with Pri could be a disaster waiting to happen. They were both hot heads, and Blind was in a semi committed relationship. But you couldn't tell two grown ass people nothing.

"Aight, man. I'll be out front waiting on you in ten minutes."

"Uh huh. Bye." I couldn't wait to get to him, so I could cuss his ass out some more.

———

Pri's House was one of those places that didn't really exist on paper, but if you were anyone, you knew exactly where to go and the hours of operation. A low-slung building on the corner of 132nd and St. Nicholas, the gambling spot was one that I had been introduced to prior to becoming the hood's medic. Back then, I wasn't entering through the side door with my med bag. I walked through the front, hanging on the arm of the same man I was now avoiding – Quan.

As we turned onto the street, the block was littered with people, and I wasn't surprised. This kind of environment thrived on adrenaline. So, I was sure that whatever had gone on inside the building only put a pause on the festivities for the night that they were anxious to get back to. Pri ran a tight ship and made sure to rub elbows within the assigned police precinct to keep their presence limited when it came to anything that wasn't within her control.

Blind sat in the passenger seat, shaking his head. "You know what happened?"

"Not yet." Parking away from the crowd, I reached for the door handle. "We'll know soon enough."

Stepping out of the car with my med bag in one hand and my phone in the other, we walked up to the side door. Pressing the buzzer twice, a man appeared at the door and waved us forward with a nod of his head. He didn't bother checking us for weapons because I always made it known that myself and whoever was with me would be protected at all times.

Inside, the air was dense with sweat, smoke, and a mixture of perfume and cologne. The scent of blood became more present as we continued down a narrow hall to the main floor of the gambling house. It was the smell of fresh blood – just enough to make your nose twitch and put you on alert. From across the room, I locked eyes with a familiar face – Lucci. His shirt was cut open, and his chest rose unevenly as he made attempts to keep his breathing steady. Fresh blood seeped through a piece of material that was tightly tied around his shoulder.

Whoever attempted to control the bleeding knew a little about first aid. By the looks on the faces of the three men with AKs, I knew they weren't to thank for the patchwork.

"Wa… wassup, Lacey?" Lucci managed to get out as I made my way over to him to survey the damage. "Quan said…"

"I said you'd be here. You're too dedicated to the people to miss the call." I heard Quan's voice nearby and froze temporarily. Stepping into view, he looked down at me. "I made the shirt as tight as I could to control the bleeding."

"Yeah. This nigga was in here actin' like Doogie Howser," Lucci joked before letting out a fit of coughs and reaching for his shoulder. "Ahhh, shit!"

"Stop talking and don't move," I instructed, completely ignoring Quan as I got to work.

"Give her some room, bruh," Blind insisted.

I glanced up briefly to see Quan nod and give me all of three and a half feet. What were the odds that I'd end up at Pri's in the wee hours of the morning, tending to Quan's cousin of all people? The universe was about to piss me clean the fuck off. I knew that much. I could feel Quan's eyes burning a hole in the side of my head as I worked, but I gave him nothing to read. Not a frown. Not a head nod. My resting bitch face activated.

Drowning everyone out in the room, I focused on Lucci. Once I got the wound cleaned, I got a better visual of what I was working with. To my surprise, I could feel the bullet that was still lodged into his shoulder.

"Blind, there's a tray in the bag. Take it out and put that alcohol in it please." While he got what I needed, I took a breath and walked Lucci through what needed to be done. "I gotta take this bullet out, and in order to do so, I need you to be still. It's gonna hurt like hell, and I don't have anything to numb the area with. Can you handle it, or do you need to go to the hospital?"

"Do what you gotta do."

"Okay." I sterilized my tools and with skillful precision removed the bullet from his shoulder.

Lucci grinded his teeth the whole time, fighting through the pain. Sweat beads appeared on his forehead, displaying just how rough it was.

"Goddamn! Can I get a couple shots of Henny or something? This shit burning like a motherfucka."

"No," I answered on behalf of those congregated.

"You cold, Lacey." He chuckled then winced. "That's why I… ahh, fuck! That's why I fuck witchu."

"Talk less. Breathe more," I muttered, not here for the pleasantries.

"I know you miss that, cuzzo," he said to Quan.

Rolling my eyes hard, I tugged on the thread I used to stitch his wound tighter than necessary. "Don't move please."

Pri finally made her appearance, stepping into the room just as I was finishing weaving the last few stitches. Her stiletto heels echoed through the room with each step she took. I could hear the rattle of the custom chain that held onto her baby, Daddy-O. Daddy-O, Pri's seventy-five-pound Doberman Pinscher, rarely left her side. The black beauty was well trained and well groomed. Pri didn't play about her four-legged son, and he would tear yo' ass up about her.

"Hey, boo," she spoke, walking over to me. "Thanks for coming. Shit got crazy fast."

"What happened?" I asked, not pausing in my work.

"Some new young niggas came through, lost big to Big Lucc, and accused him of cheating. Mix a little liquor with a lot of testosterone, niggas get to fightin'. One of the lil' niggas pulled a gun, hit Lucci, and here we are."

"And the shooter?"

"Where niggas usually go that disrespect my establishment," she replied bluntly. "How much longer? I know I'll have visitors soon, and I would like him out of here before they arrive. No offense, Lucci."

"I ain't trippin'."

"He's good," I said, placing a bandage over the newly stitched wound. "Have you been drinking?" I questioned Lucci, who shook his head no.

"Nah. I wasn't in this joint long enough to get started."

"Good. Take these pain meds. It'll help with the discomfort. You'll have to get something over the counter to help with pain going forward." Snapping my gloves off, I put them in the disposable trash bag I brought with me.

"Preciate you, Lacey. Even though you don't fuck wit cuzzo, you still came through. Even all angry and shit."

"Had I known he was here, I likely wouldn't have come at all. You got lucky tonight." I turned to Pri, who wore a smirk as she handed me a stack of bills that looked fresh out the bank.

"You always come through for me. You know I don't take it for granted."

I nodded. "I know, Pri. Have a good night. Later, Daddy-O." I rubbed the dog's head and gestured to Blind that we could leave.

"I'll call you later, Blind," Pri said to his back as he passed her with a slick grin on his face.

"Nutty and nuttier," I commented once we reached my car.

He didn't reply, just widened his grin as he hopped in on the passenger side. Before we could clear the scene, I heard my name called.

"Lacey."

"Lord, please," I said out loud, turning in time to see Quan jogging in my direction.

"What you want me to do?" Blind asked with his hand on the door, ready to step out again.

"I got it," I assured him.

"You bogus if you talk to that nigga but do you," he said with a shrug.

"I'm not gonna keep you long. I just need to say this."

Turning to face him, I leaned against my car, my body showing disinterest. "Make it quick. I gotta get home to my man. I'm playing myself by even giving you this minute. Sixty." I started a countdown in my head.

His mouth twitched, letting me know my statement hit the way I wanted it to. "I'ma eat that cause I deserve it."

"Not even close to what you deserve but go head."

"Real shit, I was deadass wrong. I threw away something solid for a maybe. That shit was dumb. You ain't deserve that. Turns out the baby isn't even mine. That bitch had been dippin' back with her ex. And felt it was best to..."

"Is that all?" I interrupted. This wasn't the closure I expected to feel. In fact, I felt nothing. Oddly, that put me at ease. "I'm glad you are walking in your truth. See, I was your lesson, NayQuan. I hope you learned it, so you don't fumble again."

He nodded, stepping back. "I'ma make it right. If it's the last thing I do," he vowed. "Whatever you got going on is temporary. I'ma let you have it for now."

"You went from apologetic to weird, but I'm not surprised. Be stressed, Quan."

Climbing inside my car, I pulled off. Blind said nothing as we drove, but I could feel his eyes on me.

"What, Brandon?" I finally spoke, not turning in his direction.

"I don't know what you think you just accomplished back there, but as a man, I think I can speak on our behalf and let you know that you just gave that nigga hope that he can get you back. You gon' see him again. Mark my words."

For the first time, I didn't have a comeback for him. This time, he may have been right, and I was deadass wrong.

<hr>

After dropping Blind off, I found myself parked in front of my building. One hand gripped the steering wheel while the other held my head up. I'd been staring off into the night, trying to figure out how I could somehow minimize the significance of my interaction with Quan to avoid telling Wizdom about it. *What he don't know won't hurt him,* I thought to myself.

But that was the easy route. The dishonest route. The route that he was very clear that I should **not** take just last night. The one that kept my world from tilting and Wiz from side eyeing me every time my phone lit up. I couldn't do that to him. It was the same shit Quan had done to me a time or three. Again, Blind's words crept in – low and cautious.

"I'm not saying you gotta volunteer everything, but I know you. You falling in love with that nigga, Wiz. Don't let that man be the last to know."

Massaging my temples, my lips tightened as I stared down at my phone that sat in my lap. On the screen was Wiz's contact photo. Would I want to know about an interaction he had with an ex? Hell yeah. I'd want to know it all – the whole damn script, tone of voice and body language included.

Sighing, I let my head hit the headrest and closed my eyes. "Damn."

In the middle of my silent battle, my phone vibrated against my thigh. It was Wiz calling. Exhaling slowly, I answered. **"Hey, baby."**

"Hey, beautiful. I got your call and your text. I was caught up in some shit. Everything aight? You good?"

His concern made my chest tighten. **"Yeah. I just made it back. About to head upstairs."**

"You sound... off. What went down on the call?"

"Had to remove a bullet. It was messy, but I handled it."

"Alright. I still have some shit to sort out here. I'll be back, but it'll be late in the morning. Hold on."

A FaceTime request came through, and I accepted the call. His face appeared clearly, but his background was dark.

"Everything okay on your end?"

"It will be. Come on, I wanna make sure you get in the house safe."

"Okay." Reaching over on the passenger seat, I picked up my med bag and got out of the car.

"Make sure to check your surroundings before you start walking. Let me see too." I flipped the camera to show him the empty street. "You didn't park in the garage?"

"Not tonight." Crossing the street, I entered my building. We were quiet on the elevator ride up until I made it inside the apartment.

"It'll be a couple hours before I make it back that way. You need anything?"

Guilt set heavy in my throat, causing a moment of silence. "No," I finally let out. "I don't need anything. I do wanna talk to you about something later though."

His head cocked to the side slightly, and his eyes narrowed. "You got my ear now, beautiful. Wassup?"

"I'd rather talk about it face to face." His brow went up, making me chuckle softly. "I mean with you physically here, Wizdom. In front of me."

"Oh, aight," he replied like he wanted to say more but let it ride. "Get you some zzz's and I'll see you in a bit. Love you."

His words stunned me. Blinking a few times to make sure I wasn't trippin', I pulled the camera closer to my face. "Wizdom, you said..."

"I said I love you."

"Well, technically you said, *love you*." I grinned wildly.

"I love you, beautiful. Get some zzz's."

"Okay. I love you too. Be safe."

I ended the call and stood in the middle of my dining room, stuck. The warm and fuzzy feeling that four letter word gave me didn't last long as the face to face I needed to have loomed in the air.

"Go to bed, Lacey," I said out loud to myself. "We got a few hours to figure this shit out."

6

WIZDOM

The called ended, and I stared at the blank screen longer than I intended. Though Lacey's voice was calm and her words were in place, I'd come to know her well. I often read her body language, and her eyes always said something. It was subtle shit I picked up on – like the way she kept pulling at the flyaway hairs that weren't contained in her bun. There was something on her mind.

I didn't want to pressure her into talking, so I didn't press the issue. Just told her what had been on my mind for the last two months. It felt right to say in the moment – reassuring. Her response was expected, seeing as I hadn't planned to say the words until they came out. Nevertheless, it felt good to know she loved a nigga back.

Getting out of my car, I walked over to Suge, who stood, leaned against her matte black Charger, in her phone. She'd traded her dress pants and button down for an all-black Nike Tech. I knew by her attire that we were about to be on fuck shit.

"Shit gotta be serious for you to take your call in the car. Everything cool with Lacey?"

"Yeah." I nodded, pocketing my phone. "Say she wanna talk to me bout some shit face to face."

"That sound deep, my boy. You know how shook y'all niggas get when a woman say she wanna talk. Get to sweatin' and shit."

"And how you get? You know, since you a nigga and shit."

She smirked. "Ion trip, bruh. I can't get nobody pregnant. And that's the only thing that will ever have me sweatin'. That and having the package. I got a feeling Lacey ain't on no shit like that." She paused and stared at me. "Oh, shit, Lacey pregnant?"

"Now why would that be your first question?"

"Shit," she shrugged, "lesbian sixth sense. You must think so too. You got that crease in your forehead you get when you thinkin' bout something serious."

"I am. I'm thinkin' bout breaking this nigga, Tim, neck for playin' wit me."

Suge nodded. "Oh, I'm witchu on that. But, trust, I already got niggas on his ass as soon as I seen the footage. I can only imagine what he look like."

"Let's get this shit over with, so I can go." The block was quiet, and none of our people were outside as expected.

We'd just opened up shop in the Bronx after Suge put me on to an open market on Matilda Avenue. Her cousin owned a house that she was having trouble renting out, and being the strategist she was, Suge convinced her to rent the place to us. Within two weeks of getting the keys, we had the spot jumping from ten a.m. to midnight. My people were used to structure, so there was clock in and out times, and we rotated a crew of six workers on a weekly basis. Of the six, Tim was the only new face.

I'd taken a chance on him despite Suge's hesitation. And to now find out that this nigga had sticky fingers had me pissed. She didn't need to verbally say *I told you so*. Her face when I pulled up said it all.

"Yo, come on. Wassup wit y'all?" I could hear Tim's voice

trembling as we entered the house and walked into the living room.

"Clear the room," I instructed to the workers present.

"Aight, Wiz. If you ne…"

"This man said clear the fuckin' room. Not talk to him!" Suge scolded Preme. "Fuck is wrong witchu niggas not following instructions? Like, one plus one not two no more? Get the fuck out!"

"You right." Preme nodded and followed his comrades out the door.

"Wiz, I swear, man. I don't know what's going on." Tim sat tied to a chair in the middle of the room with two black eyes, a busted lip, and a gash on his forehead.

"How much you take, Tim?" I questioned, ignoring his claim of confusion.

"I… I ain't take nothing, Wiz. I would never do…"

"Wrong answer." Pulling my Glock, I hit him in the face with it. Cocking it back, I pointed it at his head. "You in here playing Pinnochio and I'ma show yo' bitch ass what Goldilocks should've done to that wolf."

"I got in over my head at a dice game around my way. Ass betted. The nigga I owe knows me. I told him I ain't have it all but would have it to him tomorrow. I was gonna borrow it from the stash and flip it back before the next count."

"So, you promised my bread to the next nigga and thought you could make it up by selling my product overtime?" I questioned for clarity.

Silence.

"At least he know the question is rhetorical," Suge let out from behind me.

"Shut up, Suge," I said, still focused on Tim. "Where my money, Tim?"

He hung his head. "In my bag. In the back," he replied, defeated.

Suge went to retrieve the bookbag he always carried around and brought it back out front. Unzipping the bag, she showed me the bills that were still wrapped and appeared untouched.

"Untie him, Suge."

"Wiz, man, please. I can work this shit off."

"Nigga, you can't do a fuck thing around this trap!" My voice boomed, pissed at his audacity. "You lucky yo' bitch ass still breathing! And who's to say how long since you around here owing niggas? Fuck up out my shit."

He stood to his feet, and I could've sworn I saw a tear drop from his eyes, but I ain't have no sympathy for him. As he went to walk past me, I stopped him. "Hold on, lemme see your hands."

"Huh?"

"Hold… your… fucking… hands… out," I gritted, and he held his hands up.

BLAOW. I shot him in the left one.

"Oh, shit!" he hollered out. "You shot me!" He grabbed at his hand.

"Yeah. You needed something to remember this interaction." I took two steps forward so that I was in his face. "Come back around here again for **any** reason and I'ma make sure you fuck the city up. Am I clear?"

"Yeah." He sniffled. "I-I got you."

"Fuck outta here."

He scrambled out of the house and ran to his parked car.

"And here I was, disappointed, thinkin' you was about to let that nigga off easy," Suge said, holding the bag out to me.

"Nah, put it up. And meet me outside."

Leaving the house, I walked back to my car and got in. I could've killed Tim, but by the look on his face when he mentioned the person he owed money, I knew he was a dead man walking. I done seen niggas put on the front of plenty obituaries behind dice games. Tim wouldn't be the exception.

"You know," Suge said casually, getting in on the passenger side, "the idea of you being a dad don't sound too bad. I'll be an unctie again."

I cracked a smile. "You stupid."

"Real shit though – you ready? I mean, if it is a bun in the oven?"

I nodded. "I'm ready for whatever life throws at me, Shi'Asia. You know me well enough to know that."

She frowned. "Aight now. I know we having a heart to heart, but ain't no reason for you to be calling me by that ghetto ass name."

Suge hated her real name. The only person who still called her by her government was her mama and mine. The rest of us only did it to piss her off.

"My bad," I said with my hands up. "But yeah. It's early in the game, but I'm ready if that's what it is."

Her frown turned to a grin, and she nodded. "You always said you'd want a daughter when the time came. What was her name again?"

"Justice."

"Right. You said she'd look just like you but would be a perfect balance of you and her mama."

"Yeah. She'd be the best part of me."

"You already love Lacey, huh?"

"Told her for the first time tonight."

"Then that's what it is, man. Take my congrats in advance." She held out her hand, and we dapped it up. "Get home to your lady. I'ma bout to go smash. I mean, crash." Winking, she got out.

I waited until she was in her car, and we pulled off at the same time. My family congratulating me before we got confirmation from a test lowkey had me wanting the results to be positive. A little me running around didn't sound like a bad idea.

After leaving the trap, I didn't head straight to Lacey's. I made a detour home. I wanted to reset my thoughts and shower the day away. Arriving home, I took a thirty-minute shower and laid down for a few. I didn't even remember falling asleep but awoke to voices coming from the front of my condo. Getting up from the bed, I grabbed my phone and threw on a pair of pajama pants and a t-shirt. Sliding my feet into some house shoes, I started toward the front where I could hear Cherish and my mother in a debate about me.

"Ma, I'm tellin' you. My brother don't eat that kind of oatmeal."

"How you gon' tell me what my son eat? He grew up on the plain oatmeal. All of y'all did. Y'all only got the flavor when I hooked it up myself."

"I'm tellin' you he like the variety pack. We can bet on it."

I chuckled at Cherish always trying to hustle somebody out some money.

"How bout we make a bet that I'll kick yo' ass up and down this kitchen? Bet that."

"Bet," Cherish challenged. It got quiet, then I could hear shuffling. "Wiz! Come get your mother!" She laughed.

Turning the corner, I could see my mother chasing her around the kitchen.

"Alrightttt," she let out, winded. "You got it, Ma."

"I know I do. Hey, son." My mother greeted me with a kiss on the cheek.

"Y'all just stopped knocking, huh?"

"This one," she pointed to Cherish, "said she called, and you didn't answer."

"I ain't hear my phone ring, Bam."

Cherish looked everywhere but at us. I knew her ass hadn't called.

"You so trifling." My mother laughed. "Why you lie?"

"I ain't lie." Cherish giggled. "I went to make the call and got distracted."

"I'm sorry, son," my mother said sweetly, patting my cheek. "We bought groceries though. You want me to cook something real quick? Where's Lacey? Gotta feed my other babies too."

I shook my head, knowing that even if I didn't want to be bothered, there was no putting my mother and sister out. "She's home. I'm gonna head her way in a little bit, so you can whip something up. Oh, and both of y'all are wrong. I don't like the regular oatmeal or the variety pack. That's Keem. I like Cream of Wheat."

"Nigga, you mean to tell me I've been wasting my money on these variety boxes, and you never said a thing?" Cherish twisted her neck with her hand on her hip as she spoke.

"Nah. I've been giving them to Keem." I laughed, and my mother joined in.

"You make me sick. I ain't buying you nothing else."

I shrugged, reasoning that it wasn't a waste seeing as I didn't throw the boxes away. Cherish would find a reason to be mad anyway, so I didn't see a need to apologize. It was nothing that a $100 Cash App payment couldn't fix. Taking a seat at the island, I checked my phone for missed messages and texted Lacey.

> Me: Good morning, baby. I stopped by the crib late this morning and ended up falling asleep. I hope you slept well. Yo friend and my mama popped up on me today. Once I get rid of them, I'll be headed your way.

Setting my phone down, I watched as my mom and Cherish tag teamed breakfast and smiled. My mother was known to dote on me and Keem growing up, but the bond she shared with Cherish was special. I wanted my future daughter to have that same experience with her mom.

"Aye, lemme ask y'all something," I said, leaning back in the chair.

My mother turned around to give me her attention while whisking pancake mix in a bowl. "Wassup, son?"

"Y'all believe in closure?"

"Depends on the situation," she answered.

Cherish squinted, her hand finding her hip again. "Closure for what? And from who?"

"An ex. That nigga, Quan, popped back up."

"Quan is Lacey's ex, right?" my mother inquired.

"Yeah," me and Cherish replied.

"Okay, Phil and Lil." She snickered. "Continue, Wizdom."

"I told Lacey if she needed some kind of closure to that situation, I wouldn't stand in the way."

Tilting her head, my mother lifted a brow. "And now you don't feel that way?"

"At all. Really don't want the nigga breathing the same air as her forreal."

"Tell her that," Cherish encouraged, sounding like a supportive friend who didn't want to take sides. "She's very understanding. I'm sure she ain't tryna talk to that nigga anyway."

"Yeah. I could tell her that, but I don't wanna come off like some lame ass nigga that's concerned about the next man. Definitely don't want it to seem like I'm backpedaling."

Cherish shook her head. "Well, I don't know why you suggested that dumb idea in the first place."

"Quiet, Cherish," my mother hushed her, setting the bowl down on the counter. "You're not backpedaling. You're being honest. You thought you were okay with it, and now you're not. All you can do is tell her that, and then her response will be just that – her response. I'd rather you keep it real than to go along with something just to save face. Especially since y'all about to step into a whole new arena with this baby."

Cherish's head whipped in my mother's direction. "Baby? What baby? Not Lacey pregnant and y'all ain't tell me nothing."

"That's because we really don't know nothing for sure yet, Bam. Chill. She's taking the test some time today."

"Don't start speaking French when it comes to me," my mother interjected. "I know. It's y'all that need the confirmation."

"Oh, my God!" Cherish did her infamous shriek that made my ears hurt. Running over to me, she hugged me around my waist and bit my shoulder.

"Ouuchhh, crazy ass!" I shoved her back lightly, standing up from the chair. "Why the hell would you bite me?"

"I'm sorry," she said with her hand covering her mouth. "I'm just so excited! Wizdom, you betta do right by my friend. I'm not playing."

"That's my baby. You ain't gotta worry bout that."

"Get that test today, son," my mother pushed. "Get all kinds. Even the store brand to be sure."

"You don't sound like you're too sure of your dream, Mama," I teased.

"Oh, I know she pregnant. Just like I know ya sister is an undercover bisexual. How many pancakes y'all want?" She casually went back to whisking the pancake batter while Cherish stood with her mouth wide open.

"Bam?" I questioned with a smirk.

"Huh?" she replied with the stuck face, letting me know there was truth in my mother's statement.

"Whenever you're ready, we can talk about it."

She didn't respond, just went back to prepping breakfast.

I oversaw the preparation of breakfast while we caught up on life. Once the cooking was done, they laid out a spread of pancakes, sausage, cheese eggs, and fresh fruit at my request. While eating, Cherish threw out a few baby names that she thought would fit my child's personality. I listened to her and my mother debate back-and-forth about which names sounded better, knowing that I already had a name picked out if, in fact, Lacey and I were pregnant.

"Thanks for having us, son," my mother said as she prepared to wash the dishes we made.

"Like I had a choice." I laughed. "Leave the dishes, Ma. I'll take care of them."

"No, you didn't have a choice. But I'll make sure that **I** put in the call next time, just to make sure you're up for company." Grabbing her purse from the island, she signaled Cherish to the door.

"How you know he ain't want me to stay, Mommy?" Cherish asked, putting her shoes on.

"I don't," I answered for her. "But I love y'all though. And don't call Lacey before I make it over there."

"Man, whatever. Love you too. I won't call. Just make sure y'all call me once y'all find out."

"I got you."

Pushing her out the door, I locked it and headed for my bedroom. I had to get dressed and head to the pharmacy. We'd waited long enough. I needed to know if I was about to be responsible for a little life or not.

Walgreens was damn near empty when I walked in. That was a good thing for me. I just knew I was about to look crazy sweeping a bunch of pregnancy tests off the shelves and into my basket. For that reason alone, I didn't ask for help as I browsed the aisles. I was a man on a mission. With my basket full, I headed to the register. Once there, the clerk glanced down at the tests then back up at me with judgmental eyes.

"Is there a limit on how many tests I can buy?"

"Oh, no. No, there's no limit."

"Aight, then. Ring my shit up and stop being nosey, Miss."

Her cheeks turned beet red, but she didn't reply. With her head down, she scanned each test quickly, tossing them in a bag. "Your total is $132.64."

Swiping my debit card, I snatched up my bag and headed out. I could've said more, but I knew my limit when it came to the Karens of the world. By the scowl on her face, she was waiting for the right opportunity to get a nigga caught up.

When I made it to Lacey's, she was sitting in the living room on the phone. She looked up as I entered and silently mouthed that she was talking to her mother. Nodding, I could hear her announce my arrival.

"My mom said hey, babe."

Walking into the living room, I sat down next to her and placed the Walgreens bag in between us. She eyed the bag but didn't say anything.

"Hey. How's everything, Ms. Angel?" I spoke as she placed the call on speaker.

"Besides tryna keep Mr. Fix It in here from fixing shit, everything is quite alright with me. How are you?"

"Don't do my daddy like that," Lacey said in defense of her father.

"I can talk about my husband, girl."

"I'm good, Ms. Angel. Let Mr. Louis know if he needs help, I know a handyman that can come out for the low."

"Shoot, it can be somebody for the low or the high right about now. This man done retired, and I think he breaking shit around here just to have something to do. But hey. That's my man, and I'ma stick beside him."

"Exactly that, Ma," Lacey encouraged.

"Well, let me go. Lacey, I love you, and I'll see you at brunch. Talk soon, Wizdom."

"Love you too, Mommy."

"Have a good day, Ms. Angel."

The call ended, and Lacey pointed to the bag. "What you got there?"

"See for yourself."

Peeking inside, she glanced back up at me. "Really?"

"No better time than the present, beautiful. You ready?"

"Nope," she admitted. "But I'm gonna do it." Standing from the couch, she picked the bag up and held her hand out for me. "Come on. Since we in this together, you can stand outside the door while I get the job done."

I smiled, taking her hand and pushing forward as she made an attempt to pull me up from the couch.

"We are."

"I don't think I have enough pee for all of these tests though. Actually, one second." Handing me the bag, she went into the kitchen. "I can pee in this and just sit the tests inside." She held up a red Solo cup.

"Good thinking." As she went to enter the bathroom, I grabbed her back by her hand. "Whatever the results…"

"You got me." She completed my sentence. "I remember, baby."

I kissed her forehead and slapped her ass. "Handle the business."

Walking into the bathroom, she closed the door behind her. This shit felt like a scene out of a Lifetime movie. The only difference was that I wasn't pacing the floor. According to the tests I picked up, it only took a minute, five at the max, for results. I could hear the water running and took that as a sign that she had done her thing.

"You good, baby?" I questioned.

"Yeah. You can come in," she replied softly.

Tucking my phone away, I put my hand on the doorknob and took a deep breath. *Chin up, nigga,* I thought to myself as I pushed the door open.

She stood at the sink with one test in her hand and the

others spread out on a towel on the counter. Her eyes told it all – a mixture of anxiousness, nervousness, and a hint of excitement.

"So, it's real?" I said, peeking over her shoulder and getting a glimpse at the positive reading.

She nodded. "Very real."

And just like that, the air shifted. Her shoulders dropped, and she turned to face me with the test still in her hand.

"These results mean so much," she expressed.

"How you feel?"

"I'm kind of all over the place with my thoughts honestly. I think I'm more surprised than anything. Like, it's really official."

"Come here." Pulling her to me, I sat down on the toilet with her on my lap. "What else is on your mind? You look worried."

"I saw Quan. Last night. At the emergency call."

Cocking my head to the side, I pushed out a slow breath. "Oh, yeah?"

"Yeah. I didn't know he'd be there. I got the call directly from my associate, Pri."

I knew Pri, and I was very familiar with Pri's House. "And?"

"She needed my assistance. I got there, and someone had been shot. That someone was Quan's cousin – Lucci. I did my job, got paid, and on my way out, Quan stopped me to talk."

"And you listened?" She nodded. "Did you say anything back?"

"Not any more than I needed to say. He apologized for how things happened between us. Said the baby he thought was his wasn't. I basically said whoopty doo and that I hope he learned his lesson."

Stroking my goatee, I nodded. "Did you tell me because you knew I'd find out at some point or because you wanted to be honest."

"Both. It's something you should hear from me."

I exhaled. "You should've told me sooner. Like as soon as it happened."

"You were out handling business. It didn't seem like something that required your immediate attention."

"So, if Fallon had pulled up on me and asked to suck my dick to show how much she missed me and I declined, is that important information for you to know in the moment?"

Jumping up from my lap, she threw the test in the sink. "First off, that's two different scenarios, Wizdom. And are you tryna tell me something?"

I sat still, unmoved by her emotional shift. "Is it?"

"Yes, it is."

"They're both exes. Only difference between both scenarios is that Quan didn't ask to fuck. But the problem for me is that you gave that nigga the space to even mention the possibility. And to answer your question, no, I'm not tryna tell you anything about Fallon."

"So, you mad? You were just okay with closure the other day, Wizdom."

Standing, I shrugged. "I lied. I don't want you talking to that nigga at all. Dead the closure. Dead the thought of trying to be cordial. Dead all that shit. You pregnant with my seed, Alacea. Shit just got real."

"It's been real."

Closing the small space between us, I put my hand on her stomach. "You right, but we got ties now. For years to come."

"Are you mad at me?" she questioned with sad eyes.

"Mad, no. Do you have me fucked up? Yes, beautiful, you do. Am I willing to look past it for the sake of the good news of us bringing life into this world? Yes. But don't make me question your moves, Alacea. The worst thing you can do is have me questioning you."

"Okay," she let out, eyes glossy.

"You hungry?" I switched gears, wanting to get my mind off our first disagreement.

"Yes. I want cheesecake."

"One slice or two, beautiful?"

"Two."

"Aight. I'll go get it."

Wrapping her arms around my waist, she rested her head on my chest. "I'm sorry."

"Don't be sorry, beautiful. Be mindful. And remember you fuckin' wit' a nigga who got a few loose screws. I'll hurt something if I feel I'm being played with." Kissing her forehead, I rested my chin on the top of her head and closed my eyes. I really hoped that she took heed to my words. It was the last forewarning I planned to give.

7

ALACEA

Wizdom left, and I returned to the bathroom to gather the positive pregnancy tests. After taking a picture to send out in a group text later, I discarded the sticks and returned to the living room. Replaying our conversation, I felt like a damn fool for even mentioning that I saw Quan. I could've at least waited for the baby news to sink in. I expected him to be angry. Distant even. But what I got instead was worse – disappointment.

I didn't want Wizdom to feel like he couldn't trust me. And although he was kind of letting me off the hook this time, I was still concerned about there being some unspoken animosity later. I didn't want that. Hell, the new life we were stepping into, we didn't need it. Curling my feet under my butt, I rested my hand on my stomach.

"Pregnant." I said the word aloud like hearing it would make it sink in more. I didn't think it would really hit me until I crossed a certain threshold in the pregnancy.

I heard keys in the door and looked up to see Wizdom walking in with a bag from Sweet Tooth, my favorite bakery that was just around the corner from my place. Seeing the bag, I perked up a little.

"Please tell me you were able to get two slices." Sweet Tooth was popular for their variety of cheesecake flavors. If you weren't at the front of the line by 12p.m., you could forget about securing your slice of Heaven.

He nodded, pulling out the small, pink bakery box and opening it like it held God's gift to man. "One plain and the strawberry swirl joint you be losing yo shit over."

"Aww, bae. You made it happen. You the man."

"This is a fact."

I smiled, taking the box from him and carefully walking it over to the kitchen. I was handling precious cargo. Taking out two forks, I held one out to him. He shook his head no with a slight smirk.

"What? You don't want none? You can have some of the plain one," I offered, making it clear that the strawberry swirl was off limits.

"I want some, but I wanna eat off your fork."

Shaking my head, I put the fork back. Making his way around the island, he positioned himself behind me and kissed my neck. Slicing a piece of the cake, I fed it to him over my shoulder.

"You supposed to feed my baby first," he said while chewing.

Hearing him say the words, *my baby,* made my stomach flutter. I turned to face him with another forkful of cheesecake. Lifting me up on the counter, he took the fork from me and set it down.

"Let's talk about what's making you worry, even though you have nothing to worry about."

I took a breath. "I've been here before. Twice actually. And as you can see, I have no babies to show for either time. Two miscarriages. Once when I was nineteen. Miscarried at ten weeks. The second time wasn't too long ago. I didn't even make it to six weeks. And while it may not be the case with us, I'm skeptical of history repeating itself, ya know."

Silence settled between the two of us, one that made me a bit uncomfortable if I was being honest.

"I didn't think to mention it before," I continued. "It's two of the few moments in time that I prefer not to relive."

He used his right hand to caress my cheek and the left to massage my thigh. "Any moment that changed you at some point is a moment I want to know about. Those moments, good or bad, have shaped the woman you are, believe it or not. I just need to know if your skepticism is going to prevent you from fully embracing this pregnancy."

"It won't. I'm happy, Wiz. I just wanna be cautious."

"Fair enough. We'll start by keeping stress to a minimum."

Wrapping my arms around his neck, I nodded in agreement. "I took a picture of the tests to send out to everyone. You think we should wait?"

"Yeah. I know as soon as you hit send, they gon' blow our phones up. Right now, I wanna feed you cheesecake and talk baby names."

"Oh, I already have a name in mind for a baby girl. What you think about Sahara?"

He chuckled. "I think that goes under the list of hell no's."

"Oh, you trash for that." I laughed, slapping the back of his neck. "We're doing this, huh?"

"We're doing this, beautiful."

The rest of the day drifted by in a relaxing calm. We picked up where we left off the previous night, watching movies, snacking, connecting, and seeing who could make the other tap out first during two fuck sessions. Then there were those few times where I caught him staring at me with admiration when he thought I wasn't paying attention. It felt like he was taking in the moment, like he was trying to hold onto this version of us, right before everything changed.

We were about to be parents, a role neither of us expected to take on together so soon. Eventually, we dozed off on the couch, me nestled comfortably between his legs as he slept peacefully with one hand on my titty and the other behind his head.

It was close to midnight when I got up to go to the bathroom. That nauseating feeling had crept in the back of my throat, and I wanted to be at the toilet before anything came up. Not wanting to disturb or concern him with my dry heaving, I used the bathroom in my bedroom. Closing the door behind me, I braced myself, but nothing came up. However, the nausea was still very much present. It felt like my stomach had shifted – like it was preparing me for something to happen.

Then, I heard it. A loud thud then voices, one deep and cold that I could place as Wizdom's. And the other, tight and tense. I'd placed that voice as well, but I silently hoped that my mind was playing tricks on me. Quickly snatching the bathroom door open, my heart raced as I heard another thump. Stepping into the hallway, Wizdom's voice was steady and dangerous.

"Bitch ass nigga, I'll kill you in here."

I rounded the corner, and everything inside me stilled. Wizdom had Quan hemmed up on the wall with his arm pressed against his neck. In his other hand, there was a Glock, pressed hard into Quan's cheekbone.

"Yo, get…" Quan tried to speak but Wiz taking the safety off the Glock halted his words.

"Bae!" I rushed forward but slowed down to avoid him making any sudden movement.

Only he didn't move at all.

"What the hell are you doing in my house, Quan? Are you fuckin' crazy?!" I snapped.

"I… I…"

"Shut the fuck up," Wiz gritted, cutting him off. "Did you

know this nigga still had a key?" He finally looked back at me, eyes flashing with rage. "Lacey!" he barked, making me jump.

"No, bae," I managed to get out.

"Bet." Lowering the gun, I watched him click the safety back on.

My heart didn't stop racing though. Before I could try to get control of the situation, he brought the Glock down on Quan's face hard and commenced to pistol whipping him. Things happened so fast; I couldn't react. It didn't take long before Quan attempted to defend himself, throwing a few wild punches, only landing two.

"Yeah, bitch ass nigga. That's what I like," Wizdom taunted, sliding his gun across the floor toward me. "Fight back, pussy!"

"Wizdom, no! These white people gon' call the cops on y'all. Quan, get the hell out my house! And give me my key!" That made them stop.

Quan stumbled a little as he stood to his feet, and I pulled at Wizdom's shirt to stop him from taking off again. Blood ran down Quan's face from an open gash on his forehead, and his left cheek had begun to swell. I knew he needed medical attention and hoped that he wouldn't try to square up again because he was already on the losing end.

"I got the key," Wizdom said, pulling away from me and picking his gun up from the floor. Pointing it at Quan, he gave a final warning. "Get the fuck outta here before I paint this shit with your inner thoughts."

Bloody, defeated, and embarrassed, Quan glanced at me briefly. Everything he wanted to say was conveyed through that one glance before he let himself out.

Wizdom shook his head, jaw tight. "Here's your key." Tossing it on the dining room table as he passed, he headed to the living room.

Ensuring that both the top and bottom locks were secure, I

followed behind him. I watched as he slipped his hoodie on and stepped into his sneakers.

"Wiz," I called out to him.

"What?" he replied, not bothering to make eye contact with me.

"Where are you going?" I asked, sounding pitiful and delusional to think that he'd want to stick around after that. Judging from the way he looked up at me, he felt the same.

"You said this nigga wouldn't be a problem. Yet here I am, squabbling with him after he pops up at your crib, letting himself in with a key! Fuck is going on here?"

"I had no idea he had an extra key. We've been together for months, Wizdom. This has never happened. I've been done with him. You know that."

"Have you? Cause ain't no nigga gon' feel bold enough to just pop up unless he on the bullshit. And I know cause I'm wit the bullshit. I'ma street nigga, Alacea. Ain't no way I'm letting no man just pull up where I'm resting my head like shit sweet. If we were in a different place, I would've popped his dumb ass."

He had every right to his feelings, but what could I do? I didn't invite Quan over. I was just as pissed as him. I wanted to argue that point, but I knew it would get me nowhere.

"So, you're leaving?"

"Yeah. I need a minute. I know me, and once I'm uncomfortable, anybody around me gon' feel that shit. I'ma leave you to figure this out. Cause whether you know it or not, you done set some shit into play that you need to fix asap."

With that, he snatched up his wallet and keys from the table and walked out. Pregnancy was supposed to bring people together. This was far from that.

I sat at my dining room table after cleaning up Quan's blood, debating whether I should call Wizdom to come back or not. The battle between my heart and my ego were tussling real bad. Things felt unsettled, and the way he slammed my door when he left, it felt like a final period on a sentence that I didn't want to end. I didn't know what I expected after everything that had gone down. An argument, yes. Maybe even cold silence. But him walking away and leaving me to figure out a resolution to a situation that was a dead issue to me, no. I didn't expect that at all.

"You done set some shit into play that you need to fix asap." His words were clear, but there was nothing to fix. I couldn't make Quan act a certain way. All I could do was stay away from him after making it clear that there was no opening for reconciliation.

We didn't even get a chance to discuss how he reacted. I was still reeling from the sight of his gun pressed against Quan's cheek. The anger that radiated off him. The deadliness in his tone. That shit scared me… and turned me on at the same time. I was stuck between a rock and a hard place. I needed my girls. Picking up my phone, I started a group FaceTime call.

"Somebody better be holding you for a high ass ransom for you to be calling my phone at this time," Ashlynn said, rubbing her eyes as the call connected.

The call had connected on Cherish's end as well, but all I could see was darkness.

"Tell them to hold you til 7:30 but don't touch you. I just need a few more hours," her trifling ass had the nerve to say.

"I need y'all to come over here," I finally spoke, trying to hold back tears.

"Ho, is you crying?" Cherish questioned, flicking her light on. **"What happened?"**

"No. I'm not crying."

"Not yet she ain't but it's coming." Ashlynn pointed out.

"Cherish, get up and put something on. We'll see you in a minute, Lace." She dropped off the call but Cherish stayed.

"Where's Wizdom?"

"He left."

"It's gonna be okay, sis. We coming."

My emotions betrayed me, and a tear trickled down my cheek.

"Oh, fuck no. We coming right now!" she repeated, jumping up.

I could hear someone whisper in the background, asking where she was going. Her camera went black before she ended the call. Cherish's sneaky ass was up to something, but I couldn't even be nosey at the moment. I had my own shit to figure out.

They showed up an hour later in leggings and hoodies. Ashlynn's head was covered by a bonnet, and Cherish had on a fitted cap – dressed more for fighting than for comfort. Either way, they showed up. Neither of us spoke right a way when they entered. Ashlynn scanned the house, like she expected to see the person or thing that had me in distress, while Cherish pulled me into a tight hug – the kind of hug that said she didn't need answers yet but wanted me to know that she had me.

"I think he might be done with me," I said, voice barely above a whisper.

She pulled back slightly. "Was it that bad?"

"Quan showed up here tonight. Let himself in with a key that I didn't know he had."

Ashlynn's eyes widened. "Girl, is that nigga dumb, stupid, or slow?"

"All of the above."

"Lacey, what did Wizdom do?" Cherish asked, full of concern, her reasoning valid.

Putting my hand to my forehead, I sighed. "I heard commotion from the bathroom. When I walked out front, he had Quan hemmed up on the wall with his gun to his head. Then, he pistol whipped him. They fought a little, but Quan couldn't do anything with Wizdom. I think he was glad that I mentioned the neighbors calling the cops."

Ashlynn shook her head. "I'm sure he was. I knew his ass couldn't fight. He better be glad he walked out of here breathing."

"So, let me get this straight. My brother, Wizdom, pistol whipped Quan and let him walk outta here?"

"Yeah."

"Never thought I'd see the day or hear about it."

"The night wasn't supposed to end like this. We had just found out that..." I paused to see if I wanted to reveal the baby news now.

Cherish gave me a knowing look. "The test was positive?"

I blinked. "How'd you..."

"Me and my mom were at Wizdom's house earlier. She mentioned you being pregnant, and he mentioned you taking the test."

Ashlynn gasped. "Girl, you pregnant?"

"I am," I admitted, wiping a stray tear.

"Aww, boo. Don't cry. We keeping it, right?"

"What the hell kind of question is that, Ashlynn?" Cherish scolded. "Of course she's keeping it." She side eyed me. "You are keeping it, right?"

"Yes," I answered without hesitation.

Cherish smiled softly. "Then everything will work itself out, sis."

"We don't know that. I don't know where Wizdom's head is. He said I need to figure out where I stand with Quan. And I already know the answer to that. That ship has sailed. I just want him. I ended things with Quan the moment I saw him in that park with the baby and haven't thought about him since."

Ashlynn looked at me for a long moment. "And then he

appears out of thin air. I get where Wizdom is coming from when he told you to figure out where you stand. Think about it. You didn't mention when Quan reached out to you the first time. He found out on his own. You waited til you got a second text to block him. Then what happened at Pri's last night."

"I know. And I felt that I was doing what was best. Quan is a non-factor."

"That's what we hear you saying, but to be honest, how you're moving says differently."

"Look," Cherish spoke, "Wizdom's my brother, and I've never seen him like this about anyone or anything. Right now, I know he's not feeling you. The best thing you can do is give him space to process. If you chase him now, trying to fix it, it might make things worse."

"Yeah. It'll look like you're trying to convince yourself more than him that Quan is a non-factor." Ashlynn added. "Just fall back a little. But *if* he reaches out, which I'm sure he will since finding out about the pregnancy, be open to talking."

"Alright." Although I didn't want to, I was going to take their advice. But only for a couple days because I wanted my man back.

We ended up in my bedroom, each of us curled under throw blankets and half watching The Food Network. I appreciated their presence. It brought me some sense of comfort, even if it was brief. It wasn't long before they were knocked out, and I still found myself up, staring at the ceiling, thinking about Wizdom. Reaching for my phone, I went to text him, only to find that he had already messaged me. My previews were off, so my heart thumped as I opened our text thread. It shattered when I read the message.

Dada: We need to make an appointment with your GYN for the baby. Let me know when you set it up and I'll be there.

"Let me know when you set it up and I'll be there?" I repeated out loud. I read the message again and came up with the same interpretation.

Things had taken a turn, and this was the kind of stress I didn't need. Locking my phone, I decided against responding to the text. I needed sleep. Sleep would bring clarity and ensure that I didn't move on emotion. Because at the moment, I felt like fuck Wizdom and double fuck Quan for even putting me in this position.

8

———————

WIZDOM

I woke up the next morning, still heated about the bullshit that occurred a few hours ago. The shit Quan pulled had a nigga on the cusp of a crash out. When I left Lacey's house, I was hoping he was still in the vicinity, just so I could beat his ass some more. I even drove around the block twice just to be sure. You know how pissed you gotta be to drive around looking for someone and don't even know what kinda car they in? That was how fucked up he had me.

For the first time since we'd been together, sleep didn't come easy. I was tired. Not tired in a way that sleep could fix though. I was tired from overthinking. Saying nothing was easy. Acting like it never happened would be easier – if I didn't have real feelings for Lacey. But I loved her, and that was what made shit complicated – that and the child **we** were now expecting.

I meant what I said about her figuring out where she really stood with Quan. It was the sole reason why I had to put some distance between us. The last thing I wanted to do was look at my girl different or worse, question her moves.

"This shit crazy," I said out loud.

If there was one thing I vowed to never be, it was in my feel-

85

ings about a woman. It was a dangerous place to be, especially for a nigga like me – a nigga who wasn't wrapped too tight and had the ability to turn my feelings off in a millisecond. It was the one quality that my mother still encouraged me to work on 'til this day. I was starting to feel like my relationship with Lacey was going to force me to do that.

Reaching for my phone, I checked to see if she had responded to the text I'd sent before I went to sleep. She hadn't. Her read receipt showed that she'd seen it though. I didn't take into consideration how the message could've been perceived once I sent it. I just wanted her to know that the altercation didn't change the news we'd received. We still had to check on the life we created.

I stared at our text thread for a few seconds before locking my phone and heading for the kitchen. I wasn't hungry, but there was no telling when I'd stop to eat once my day started rolling. It was best to take advantage of my downtime now. Checking the fridge, I decided to whip up a spinach, mushroom, and Swiss omelet. In the middle of pretending that I actually knew what the hell I was doing, I heard a knock at my door.

I knew who it was before even asking. Suge's signature knock was the *Grindin'* beat by Clipse. She didn't believe in quiet anything. Taking my time walking to the door, I pulled it open just as she went to switch up the tempo.

"Oh, you must've known I was about to hit that *Doo Doo Brown* beat. Have this bitch jumpin' early like Uncle Luke."

Not only was Suge at my door, but so was Keem. They were both dressed casually in sweats and hoodies like they had nowhere to be.

"Cherish sent us," Keem said, pushing the door open and letting himself in.

Suge followed suit. While Keem headed for the fridge like he paid bills, she flopped down on my couch. The open floor plan made it so that she could be seen from the kitchen.

"She said you crashed out at Lacey's last night."

Closing the door, I went back into the kitchen. "So, what? She called y'all to check on me? Cause that shit ain't necessary. And for the record, I ain't crash out. Y'all would've known that. What she say happen?"

Keem casually cracked my last three eggs in a bowl and whisked them. "Something about Quan poppin' up and you backing out on him. Where you keep the salt and pepper?"

"Nigga, I was about to make an omelet. Fuck is you doing?"

"You mean you was about to fuck an omelet up? Cause you know yo' ass can't cook. I'ma scramble these, and we can split it," he bargained.

"Trying to compromise, in someone house, about they shit is a whole new level of audacity." Suge laughed.

"Have the eggs, bruh. Salt and pepper in the cabinet to your right." I shook my head. "Anyway, Cherish need to tell the whole story if she gon' report. I almost blew that nigga head off." Seeing as Keem had helped himself to my breakfast, I grabbed a protein shake from the fridge and went to sit in the armchair across from Suge.

"Oh, she told us that too. I was surprised you ain't pop that nigga. We could've figured out what to do with the body later. Pulling up at my woman crib late night is too crazy," Suge expressed.

"Fuck that," Keem let out. "A nigga gotta see me for pulling up at all. And wit' a key? Wooo! A nigga would be ready to take the mugshot."

"Ya feel me," Suge cosigned.

"If this is y'all way of tryna calm me down or make sure I'm good, y'all niggas are failing miserably."

Suge looked over at Keem, who shrugged and turned to the stove. "How did Lacey react? Did she try to get in between y'all?"

"Not pregnant with my seed. She better not had tried to step in and break shit up."

Suge grinned, showing the two diamonds in her teeth. "So, it's official?"

"Yeah, man." I smiled. "We found out yesterday."

"Mama was right again, I see." Keem walked over with a plate of scrambled eggs, toast, and a glass of orange juice. "Congrats again, bruh."

"Damn. This nigga got a kid on the way. That man didn't just come to ya girl house. He came to ya baby mama house. You know how niggas feel bout they baby mama. You got ta kill that nigga, Wiz. Or say the word and I can get him gone."

"Nah. Now that it's official that Lacey is pregnant, that's where his focus needs to be. He don't need to be on the bullshit," Keem reasoned while chewing.

"I'm really still wrapping my head around this whole thing. I told her she had some shit she needed to figure out. She insisted that there's nothing to figure out since she basically already chose me to lock in with. But it's like does that nigga know?"

"She can't really do nothing wit' a nigga that's persistent, bruh." Keem answered my rhetorical question.

"Kill him," Suge insisted, sounding like Chris Tucker on *Friday*.

"Man, don't listen to this lady."

"Aye, watch that shit, Keem."

I snickered, knowing at any point this whole intervention could go left if they started going at it.

"I'ma let the nigga make it… for now."

Suge shook her head. "And Lacey?"

"I sent her a text when I got home. Told her to make a doctor's appointment and to hit me with the details when it's done. I'm not in a rush to be up under her. I need a minute."

Keem nodded. "I guess that's mature. And fair."

"Sounds like a man in love to me." Suge pointed out. "I

wanna reach that level of maturity one day. When the right woman comes along, I'ma let y'all know."

Keem cut his eye at her. "We gon' get to that in a minute, Shi'Asia."

She picked up a throw pillow, and I stopped her before she could toss it. "If anything spills, I'm charging you."

"You lucky I know this penny-pinching ass nigga is serious." Setting the pillow down, she gave Keem the finger.

"I do love her. Which is why I'm giving her grace this time. For that reason and because I know she didn't know he'd pop up like he did. And I know for sure she ain't know the nigga had a spare key."

"Exactly. And I hope you stick to knowing that. Because I know you and you don't give a motherfucka an inch of grace. Just remember not to be so prideful that you fuck around and lose a good woman."

"I got this," I assured him. I'd already made up in my mind that I wasn't walking away from Lacey. This was my cool down period.

"Aight, now that we got the intervention out the way," Keem turned to Suge, "when you and Cherish start scissoring?"

Suge blinked, caught off guard. "Scissoring?"

"She a touch me not, bruh," I said to Keem.

"A touch me not," Keem repeated. "The fuck is that? Some new lesbian term?"

"Nah. It's…"

"Y'all niggas ain't gon' talk about me like I ain't sittin' right here," Suge interrupted, sitting up straight on the couch.

"Aight. So, answer the question then," Keem pushed. "And don't lie either. I saw the way y'all were at the dinner. Whispering shit to each other. Gazing into each other's eyes and shit. Wiz saw it too."

I put my hands up and shook my head. "Wiz ain't seen shit. Don't put me in that."

"Well, Detective Nosey As Fuck," Suge smirked, "to answer your question, no we ain't scissoring. We make love though."

The room went quiet. My mother was right once again.

"Damn," I let out. "Mommy don't miss at all. She just said the other day that Cherish was an undercover bisexual. Shit, if girls her thing, then I'd rather it be with you than anyone else. You got my blessing." I held my hand out, and Suge dapped me up.

"You mad, bruh?" she asked Keem, who sat in deep thought.

"Nah. I'm confused."

"About what?" I inquired.

"How this shit went over my head. But then again, Cherish ass is sneaky. And you," he pointed at Suge, "you secretive as fuck."

"Cherish ain't sneaky. Cherish ass is confused. I had to dead all that shit the night of her dinner though. That nigga, Keyon, ain't come through… yet again, and who came to the rescue? Me. And we've been playing this game for too long. I made my intentions clear and let her know that I'm not playing second for nobody while she figures her shit out. It's either me or nobody."

"You mean you or Keyon," I corrected.

She stared at me blankly. "No. I meant me or nobody. I just told you I aspire to be at your level of maturity one day. I ain't there yet. Niggas will be in the city morgue fuckin' wit' me."

"At least I ain't gotta worry bout her being protected if we ain't around. You got my blessing too." Keem dapped it up with her and finished his eggs.

They stayed for another hour to chop it up. I made sure to bring up Ashlynn since Keem seemed to have an opinion about everyone else. Of course he was still hush about his relationship status, but we all knew the real.

"Aight, I'm outta here, man," he announced. "Gotta go pick up Dooty and AJ."

"Look at you. Already got two kids and I'm still working on one." I chuckled.

"Yeah. Be thankful that you ain't gotta deal with an ex-husband/ baby daddy. This nigga got Pooh beat when it comes to irritation. The thing I like about Ashlynn is she check that shit and don't let it dictate how we move."

"Teamwork. I fuck wit that."

"Fasho. See y'all later."

"Hol' on. Take Young Suge witchu," I said, pointing at Suge, who'd taken her shoes off and laid out on the couch.

"Nigga, shut up. Y'all had me up early to play Iyanla Vanzant. I'ma bout to take a nap and dip when I'm good and ready. Lata, Keem."

Keem shrugged and proceeded out the door. Locking it behind him, I headed for my bedroom but not before taking a pillow and hurling it at Suge on my way there.

"I'ma kick yo ass, nigga!" she yelled but didn't bother getting up.

Having them put things into perspective helped because they understood both sides. Cherish had actually did a good thing by sending them over. I went to text her to thank her for her good deed when a text notification popped up from Lacey.

Beautiful: Appointment is scheduled for Monday at 2pm. I'm having brunch with our moms that day. You can meet me after.

I didn't know what kind of response I was expecting, but I didn't like that it was flat. Kind of similar to the message I sent her. Different than how we normally communicated. Had this bitch ass nigga, Quan, driven a wedge between us already? Suge might tell a joke, but she never told a lie. I just might have to pop this nigga after all.

BEFORE I KNEW IT, THE WHOLE DAY HAD GONE BY, AND I HADN'T left the house. I didn't even press Suge to leave. She had people in place at our spots, and I trusted her enough to oversee things if she wasn't in the field. I hadn't heard from Lacey all day, and that bothered me. I was used to texting or being on the phone with her throughout the day. Putting the fact that we were clearly at odds to the back of my head, I sent her a text.

> Me: What you ate today?

> Beautiful: Food.

Her response made me laugh out loud. Women could be so petty.

> Me: Can you send me a picture of your belly?

> Beautiful: It looks the same as it was when you left outta here. It hasn't grown in hours.

> Me: Aight. I love you. Get you some rest.

I thought spinning it on her and saying something nice would change her mood. But I knew the Lacey I'd come to know would have some slick shit to say when she was mad.

> Beautiful: I'll go to sleep when I'm ready. Thank you very much. I love you too.

Grinning, I went to put my phone down when it rang in my hand. I didn't recognize the number, but it was late, so whoever was calling must've known me. There weren't many people who had my personal number. I answered on the third ring.

"**Who dis?**"

"**Wiz?**" The voice on the other end was shaky, but I recognized it immediately. "**Wiz. It's Fallon.**"

"When I block people, they usually take the hint." I sighed. "What you on, Fallon?"

"Wizdom, I wouldn't be calling you if I didn't really need your help. I'm in Trenton."

"Jersey?"

"Yes. At the Double Tree hotel. Your number is the only number I know by heart. I'm using someone else's cell. Can you please come and get me?"

I rubbed my temple, conflicted. I was used to Fallon being cool, calm, and poised. This person on the other end of the phone sounded scared and anxious.

"Real shit, Fallon, I don't need you getting me mixed up in nothing. The people can't help you at the front desk?"

"No," she whispered and sniffled. "Please, Wizdom."

"Send me the address."

She read off the address quickly. "I'll text it too. I'm gonna be in the lobby. Please come."

I held the phone in my hand and stared at the wall, thinking about the shit I'd just allowed myself to get sucked into. I wasn't Super Save A Ho. I damn sure didn't need to play the role at a time when me and my woman were on the outs. Hearing the distress in her tone, along with the fact that I didn't have any beef with Fallon, was the only thing that got me to throw on some clothes. That was the first step though. I needed perspective in order to get me out the door. I headed to the living room where Suge was sprawled out on the couch. She had a sandwich in one hand, the remote in the other, and her phone pressed to her ear.

"I told them, so you ain't have to. Ion care if..." she paused, noticing me. "Hold on, Cherish. Where you..." I cut her off, shaking my head, and gestured for her to hang up. "Lemme call you back, bae." Ending the call, she set her sandwich down. "What's good?"

I explained the call from Fallon and watched as Suge's expression shifted from curiosity to disbelief.

"So, she sound scared, and you were the one person she thought to call?" she asked. "That shit sound weird."

"I said the same thing. I'm on the fence about it. Granted, I'm not on that typa time with Fallon anymore, but what if shorty really is in trouble?"

"True. But before you make your final decision, there's something you might need to know about Fallon."

I blinked. "What?"

"Shorty sell pussy. Got an OnlyFans page and all."

I ran my hand over my face. "Why you just now saying something?"

"I thought I did once. Maybe it went over your head. And I knew you weren't serious about her, so I thought fuck it, it's your turn."

I chuckled at her comment because if Suge wasn't born with female parts, I would've sworn she was a man just by her thought process alone.

"So, you think I should say fuck it and wish her the best?"

Reaching over on the table, she took the last bite of her sandwich and stood up. "Nah. You should take me with you. That way, I have your back in the event shit go left."

"Bet. Let's go." I started for the door and stopped. "Wait."

"What?"

"Suge, when this girl get in the car, don't start clowning. We picking her up and dropping her off."

"Aight. I'ma be serious."

"I'm deadass."

"Me too, nigga. I know how to conduct myself around a call girl."

"Suge!"

"Aight. I got that one out. I'm done."

Shaking my head, I kept walking to the door.

"You drive," I said once we made it outside.

"Keem was my ride."

"Damn." I'd hoped that I could make this shit less complicated by not having Fallon in my car. I was doing too much as it was. "Come on."

In the car, I typed in the address that Fallon texted me. The ride to Trenton had a nigga on edge. Every time we passed an exit, I contemplated getting off and heading back home. I just had a feeling that Lacey would call at any moment, and then, there'd be nothing I could say to her that wasn't the truth.

"Nigga, is you sweating? We can just turn back if it's making you do all that. Fallon ain't your responsibility."

"I'ma have to tell Lacey about this."

"About what?"

"About this shit. What I'm about to do."

"I don't know what you talkin' bout, bruh. We just best friends taking a drive. That's the story. Stick wit' it."

I didn't reply, just kept driving with Lacey heavy on my mind. When we arrived at the hotel, I pulled up to the side and kept the engine running.

"You want me to go in there and get her?" Suge offered, taking her seatbelt off.

"Yeah."

I watched as she got out, did a quick scan of the area, and then walked into the hotel. Seconds later, she reemerged with a worn-out looking Fallon. Her eyes darted around the parking lot, and she looked disheveled. Fallon always had on a designer fit, but the bodysuit she wore was straight off the mannequin at Pretty Girl. Suge led her to the car, opening the back door and helping her inside.

"Wizdom." Her voice trembled. "I..."

"Before you continue," I cut her off, "is someone looking for you?"

She shook her head no.

"Whose phone did you call from?"

"The janitor let me use his phone."

"Aight. I'ma take your word for it. That's all you have with me, Fallon."

"I know."

"What happened?"

"I was on a… a date. The guy got rough with me and robbed me. I couldn't call anyone else."

Suge glanced over at me and mouthed, prostitute.

Shaking my head, I confirmed that we were dropping her home and headed that way. The drive to her place was silent. When we arrived, she leaned forward from the backseat.

"Thank you, Wizdom."

"Be safe, Fallon. But don't hit my line again."

Nodding sadly, she got out of the car. Once she was in the building, I peeled off. We were a block away before Suge finally spoke.

"That was some noble, gangsta shit you did. I hope it don't come back to bite you in the ass."

Though I'd heard her words loud and clear, my eyes stayed fixated on the road to avoid pushing her ignorant ass out the car. How the hell did me needing space end up with me taking Lacey's wrong and doubling up? This shit was wild.

9

ALACEA

I just knew when I prayed to God last night over my baby, my life, and my relationship that I was clear on what I wanted. Another bout with morning sickness wasn't on the prayer list. Yet I was making my second mad dash to the bathroom, barely getting to the toilet in time. I didn't even think morning sickness was the right phrase anymore. This was all day madness.

I leaned over the sink to brush my teeth and attempted to gather myself. Today, I was supposed to have brunch with my mother and Ms. Angela, but with my stomach doing gymnastics, there was no way I could make it through an outing comfortably. I hated to cancel on them, especially after having delivered the baby news yesterday in a group text. I knew they'd want time to fawn over me. After taking care of my breath, I picked up my phone and dialed Ms. Angela's number.

"**Hey, honey,**" she greeted in a warm voice.

"**Heyyy. Did I call too early?**" I looked over at the clock on my wall, and it was 8:45 a.m.

"**No. You're good. I've been up since six. Everything okay?**

"I'm okay overall, but this morning sickness has me down bad. I'm sorry. I won't be able to make brunch today."

"Oh, girl, I remember those days. And don't be sorry. Do you need me to come over? I can bring you some ginger ale and crackers. Or better yet, where's Wizdom?"

I rolled my eyes at his name. "He's home. We have a doctor's appointment this afternoon, so I'll see him then. And no, you don't have to come over. I'm gonna make myself some tea and lay back down."

"Alright. Well, you call me if you need me, okay? And not just for the baby. For that son of mine too."

"Will do. I'd still like to treat you and my mom to brunch if you're still up to going."

"I sure am. I love to dine on someone else's dime."

"Same." I laughed. "I'll have my mom give you a call. Enjoy."

Next, I dialed my mother and gave her the same spiel. Unlike Ms. Angela, she was trying to force her way over to take care of me. After convincing her for the third time that I was good and would check in after my appointment, she finally let me hang up the phone.

Settling back in bed, I thought to call Wizdom, but after two days of not having a real conversation with him, I felt like calling would give off the impression that his lack of communication was okay. And it was anything but that. It was not just because this hadn't been an issue for us thus far, but we'd discussed that shutting down on each other wouldn't be an option in the relationship. However, we'd managed to let this Quan situation get the best of us. I hated it. Annoyed, I put a pillow between my legs and had started to force myself to sleep when the doorbell rang.

I wasn't used to getting visitors this early. Thinking it might be Wiz trying to be funny by not using his key, I got up to answer it. I was surprised to see my brother on the other side of the door, holding my niece in a car seat.

"Surprise!" He grinned, and I instantly teared up. "Mann, don't start that crybaby ass shit, Alacea."

"Shut up and come inside." I pulled him in by his shirt. "Hurry up and take her out. She wants me. Come on Aunty Maya."

In the car seat, Amaya excitedly kicked her shoeless feet in the air and blew spit bubbles. Lance was taking too long for me, so I went in and scooped her up myself. Her baby smell instantly soothed me.

"Heyyy, big girl. Oh, my God, Lance. She smells so good."

"Should've smelled her earlier. Straight trifling." He laughed, following us into the living room.

"Shut up. My niece don't stink." We sat down, and I couldn't help but to smile at Amaya cooing and giggling. I checked out her little two-piece skirt set she had on that matched her hair bow. "You cute, niece." I smoothed out her skirt. "What y'all doing over here so early?"

"She has a doctor's appointment at ten thirty. Figured since she was already up and the doctor's office not too far from here, we'd stop by. Wassup witchu? How are things?"

I sighed. "Me and Wizdom beefing."

"Why?"

I ran down the situation with Quan and how things had played out leading up to the fight with him and Wizdom.

Lance shook his head. "I'm surprise he let that nigga live. Quan would've had to go have his spot in Heaven off the pop up alone. That is wild, Lace."

"I know."

"Men like Wizdom have a lot of pride. You gotta be upfront always. He gotta look over his shoulder enough wit the business he in. How he feel about the baby?"

"He's happy. I'm happy too but..."

"Nah. Don't do that. Be happy. There's no buts. Like Mommy said, God makes no mistakes."

"You're right. You think I'ma have a girl?" I asked, glancing down at Amaya.

"For the sake of Wiz's pockets, I hope not."

"You might have a point there, brother." We both laughed.

He caught me up on a few of Amaya's milestones before they had to leave for her appointment.

"I love y'all," I said, walking them to the door.

"We love you too," Lance replied lovingly, kissing my cheek. "And just so you know, I'm pulling up on that nigga, Quan, today. If Wiz already hasn't."

"La..."

He shook his head. "Your way ain't working, Lace. Clearly this nigga ain't getting the hint. So, now we gotta force it. Send me a message and let me know how the appointment goes."

"Alright," I conceded.

Between Lance and Wizdom, I was going to let them handle Quan as they saw fit. It was evident that my way of saying *leave me the hell alone* wasn't working. It was a weight on my shoulders that I didn't need anyway. Hell, I was just a girl. A pregnant one at that.

My phone ringing next to my ear pulled me from a peaceful sleep. The chamomile and peppermint tea mixture I'd concocted to settle my stomach put me right out on the couch. Picking up the phone with my eyes closed, I answered.

"**Beautiful,**" Wizdom's voice came through, "**our appointment is in an hour. You getting ready?**"

"**Oh, shoot,**" I said, checking the time. "**I went back to sleep and didn't set an alarm.**" Popping up, I rushed to my room.

"I'm gonna freshen up real quick, and I'll be ready. Let me send you the address."

"That won't be necessary. I'll be there to pick you up, so we can ride together."

I paused.

"That cool witchu?"

"Yes. That's fine," I replied, trying to sound uninterested, knowing I was happy as hell. I missed his presence. But I wasn't ready to tell him that. He had to say it first.

"I'll see you in a few. I love you."

"I love you too." Close to breaking my cool girl act, I hung up first.

With my doctor's office being twenty-five minutes away from my house, I freshened up quickly and threw on a pair of ripped mom jeans. I went to pull my graphic tee over my head and stopped to look in the mirror. To now know that the weight I'd been gaining was due to me creating life made me blink back tears.

"Somebody's fine ass mama," I said aloud, pulling the shirt down.

Hitting my body with a couple spritzes of Kay Ali Vanilla 28, I slipped my feet into my Prada sneakers and grabbed a jean jacket from the closet. Although the sun was out, I liked to have something to cover my arms in the event it got a little breezy. As I made my way to the kitchen to grab a snack for the ride and a bottle of water, I could hear keys in the door. I stopped short when it pushed open and Wizdom walked in.

"Wassup, beautiful?" he said coolly.

"Hey." My feet stayed planted.

"My mama called and said you were having a rough time this morning. I bought you some ginger ale and crackers. I also picked up these prenatal vitamins. I didn't know which ones to get, so I used that Yuka app you made me download, and I got these."

I watched as he pulled the items from the bag and held up the vitamins. He was making it real hard to stay mad doing all this conscious daddying. Then got the nerve to be looking good as fuck. The white tee he had on was fitted, and his arm tattoos were on display. His jeans sagged just right, and he had on the same sneakers as me. To top it off, I could tell he'd just come from the barbershop. It was given, he needed to stay his ass in the house while I checked on the baby. Composing myself, I slowly walked over to him to check out the vitamins.

"How did they scan on the app?" I asked, not making eye contact.

"83 outta 100. I didn't know if the doctor would prescribe you some, so I just got the one box. You ready to go?"

I nodded. "I'm gonna grab a water and my grapes." Taking the ginger ale and crackers, I put them both away. "Alright, let's go."

The car ride was quiet at first, but then he reached over and picked up my hand.

"Why didn't you call me and tell me you were still struggling with the morning sickness? I text you to check in, and you haven't mentioned it."

"I didn't call because I'm not interested in having a forced conversation with you."

"What you mean?"

I took my hand from him and crossed my arms. "You just said you text me to check in. That's not even us, Wizdom. We've been with each other almost every day since making it official. How we go from that to you just checking in on me? You don't find that crazy?"

"It's unfortunate. And I don't want you to think a nigga been at the crib throwing a party. I've been in the streets and straight home, getting my mind right. That Quan shit affected me more than I let on. I guess it's more so me knowing the bullshit you went through and trying to understand why he would pop up now. I mean, I know you ain't summon him but still. The way shit played out, it was best for me to take that space."

"I've been missing you, but I didn't know how to tell you. All I know is that the bed felt different without you in it. I don't wanna lose you, Wizdom."

Arriving at the office, he parked and turned to me. "You haven't run a nigga off, beautiful. I'm here. I apologize for checking out on you. That was wrong. I'm just used to getting the fuck on when I'm in a situation that puts me in a bad space. But we were clear that we would do things different together. So, you have my word that that won't happen again, aight?"

"Okay. I scheduled an appointment with maintenance to change the locks tomorrow. I never want you to feel uncomfortable when you come over. I want my place to still bring you peace."

He stared at me for a few seconds before speaking. "When's your lease up?"

"Ummm, I believe in two months. Why?"

"Break it and move in with me. Don't worry bout the cost. I'll cover it."

"Break it? I like my place, bae."

"We'll find you something better if moving in with me isn't something you wanna do right now. I gave it some thought, and I don't feel comfortable with you staying there after what happened. Shit, I didn't feel comfortable when I left. I actually had my people watching your building the last two days just for my peace of mind."

"Are you sure? You've never lived with a female other than Cherish, Wizdom. I have a lot of stuff."

"And I have a lot of space. I'm kinda not taking no for an answer either. I didn't wanna just come right out and say that though."

"What if I say yes and you find yourself tired of me and wanna put me out or what if I just up and wanna leave?"

He chuckled. "What if you say yes, and I never get tired of you? What if you never wanna leave? I've done enough negative thinking these past two days. Let's think positive."

Smiling, I kissed his lips. "Okay. I'm on board."

"Good. Let's go check on our lil' one."

NORMALLY, THE WAIT TIME TO SEE MY DOCTOR WAS LONG, BUT today things seemed to move quickly, and I was grateful. As soon as I stepped into the building, my nerves got the best of me. I hadn't logged my last period, so I wasn't sure how far along I was. I just hoped that I was past the ten week mark. Even if it was by a few days, I knew that hearing that news would really put me at ease.

Sitting on the exam table, I swung my legs, glancing over at Wizdom every now and then. He sat chillin' in the corner, ever so calm. His eyes occasionally scanned the room before landing on mine and giving me a reassuring nod.

"We good, beautiful," he said, voice low and smooth.

"I know," I replied quickly.

He smiled a little – not big, just enough. "Good. Cause ain't nothin' to stress about. We just checkin' in on beautiful jr."

"Beautiful jr?" I laughed.

"Yeah. I got a good feeling that it's a girl."

I blushed. "I'm sure we won't find out today."

"That's cool. I just wanna make sure she healthy and growing."

His positive energy settled my nerves. I needed that.

"Knock, knock." My doctor entered the room with a smile as big as Wizdom's when the nurse confirmed my positive pregnancy test. "I see we're back with amazing news."

"Yes, we are." Wizdom spoke on our behalf.

Dr. Mallory laughed and turned to Wizdom. "Sounds like Dad."

"The one and only," he said proudly.

"Oh, I like him, Alacea."

Dr. Mallory was cool. She'd been my OB since I was sixteen and knew my coochie like the back of her hand. She'd encouraged me through my miscarriages, reminding me that losing babies didn't make my chances of conceiving one day slim. It would happen when God saw fit. I hoped that this go round was that time.

"Alright, my girl. Let's check you out and see how far along you are with the lil' bean."

I laid back on the table, and she squeezed that cold gel on my stomach. I jumped a little, making Wizdom stand up from the chair and post up at my side. The screen on the ultrasound machine flickered on, and she maneuvered the probe around until a little body popped up. Our lil' one was stretched out like he or she was in mid nap.

"Looks like the lil' one is relaxed, huh?"

I grinned while Wizdom grabbed hold of my hand and squeezed it. "Damn," he whispered. "She's mine."

"You're being that dad already?" I joked.

He kissed my lips and smiled. "We can share her, beautiful. That's my baby tho."

"Whatever." I giggled. "How far along am I, Dr. Mallory? Please tell me I'm past the ten-week mark."

"Congrats, honey. It looks like we're thirteen weeks today with a due date of November 24th. Baby is the perfect size, heartbeat is perfect and strong. You wanna hear?"

We nodded. She pressed a few buttons and turned two knobs. I held my breath, releasing it once my baby's heartbeat filled the room. Unable to contain myself, the tears flowed freely down my face.

"Wow," I let out, in awe.

"Justice," Wizdom said. "Her name is Justice."

"We have another five weeks before we can tell the sex. I love your confidence though, Dad."

She printed out the sonogram pictures, congratulated me, and threw in an I told you so followed by a genuine smile. With a prescription called in for prenatal vitamins, we made our way back to the car. My mind was at ease. Me and Wizdom were back, and we had a healthy, growing baby on the way. All that was left to do now was a pregnant woman's favorite pastime – eat.

<hr>

"She got your forehead, bae." Wizdom pointed out, examining the sonogram pictures for the third time since we arrived at the restaurant.

"Oh, please." I laughed, nudging him with my elbow. "My forehead cute."

"That's what I meant." He kissed my head. "Cute as hell."

"I don't wanna know the gender when the time comes. I wanna be surprised." Taking a bite of my chicken caesar wrap and held it up for him to take one.

"You wanna do that gender reveal thing all the women be doing?"

I nodded, grinning. "Yup. But ours won't be like everybody's."

"Whatever you wanna do, bae. Anything for the queen and our princess."

"Oh, you got this daddy thing down pat already. I love you."

"Show me. Chew that food and open your mouth."

"You are unbelievable," I said, taking another bite of the wrap and opening my mouth after two chews.

Like a bird, he ate the minced food and sat back with a satisfied smile. "I'm glad I was able to be there with you today. You gotta know that no matter what we go through, I'm always gonna show up for our baby."

"How about we agree not to do anything that would put us in a position where you just show up for our baby? I like that better than what you said."

"Yeah. What you said, beautiful. Moving forward, no surprises."

Right on cue, the universe showed us how hilarious it could be.

"Hey, Wizdom. Please excuse my intrusion."

My head snapped up first, and my eyes narrowed, placing the face of the woman immediately. I expected for Wizdom's demeanor to change. That way, I had something to go on, but the look on his face said that he was anything but fazed by her presence. I forced myself to appear the same way, even though I was steaming inside.

"Fallon, right?" I said, and she nodded to confirm. "In case you haven't noticed, this is a party of two."

"Three, beautiful," Wizdom corrected, pointing to the sonogram that sat next to him on the table. He took a slow sip from his orange juice and glanced up at Fallon.

That calm shit was pissing me off, and the fact that the knock off Keri Hilson was still standing in front of our table looking sad and dumb was sending me to the moon.

"Fallon, if you love them people that live at 3110 Lexington Ave, I suggest you move from this table. It's not safe here. Trust me when I tell you," Wizdom threatened.

"I..." She didn't get a chance to finish before I tossed his orange juice in her face.

Cutting my eyes at Wizdom, I snatched up my bag. "Please wrap up my food. I'll be outside."

I knew I was in no condition to be fighting, but I still made sure to bump the shit out of Fallon and call her a punk ass bitch as I walked past her and out of the restaurant.

Pulling out my phone, the first number I thought to dial Cherish. I heard Wizdom behind me before I could.

"Before you get on the phone bashing a nigga, can we talk first?"

Turning, I mean mugged him. "Oh, I plan to do both. But first, lemme introduce myself. Hello, Pot, I'm Kettle." I held my hand up, and he grabbed it, spinning me around and guiding me to the car with his hand on my back.

Securing me inside and placing my bag of food in my lap, he got in and pulled off without saying a word. Whether he was using the silence to try to figure out what to say or giving me a minute to cool down, I took it as him being nonchalant. And that'a the last thing he needed to be. I was about to click out.

With the silence further riling me up, I spoke first. "You back fucking with Fallon again?" I asked straight up.

"No."

"So, what was that back there? Her going out her way to speak and shit."

"I helped her out the other night. She called and said she was in trouble."

Folding my arms across my chest, I turned so that my back was against the window, and I could look directly at him. "I didn't know you applied to become a 911 dispatcher. If the bitch was in trouble, she could've called 911, a family member, shit, Ghostbusters for all I care. Why she call you?"

"I couldn't even tell you forreal. I picked her up, dropped her off home, and told her not to contact me again."

The car stopped in front of his building. He parked but kept it running.

"So, after…"

"Yes. After I made it clear how you were wrong, I went and did the same shit with Fallon."

"No. You did worse, Wizdom. And had we not seen her

today, I wouldn't have known. Now we're right back to square one." Shaking my head, I sat back in my seat.

"You know what I think? I think somebody somewhere is praying over some candles, tryna tear us apart."

I tried to hold in my laugh, but I couldn't. "Wiz, please. I don't wanna joke with you."

"No, deadass. Think about it. We've been doing good from the time we locked in, and now, out of the blue, our exes make sudden, random appearances."

"Well, whatever whoever is doing, it seems to be working."

He raised a brow. "So, you tryna break up wit a nigga?"

Sighing, I shook my head. "That's not what I said."

"It's what you implied," he countered.

We both went silent.

"Do you need some kind of closure to what you and Fallon had?"

"Hell naw," he replied quickly. "We ain't had nothing remotely that deep."

"Alright. If we can move past the Quan situation, I'm willing to move past this. But this is the only pass I'm giving. I done let too much shit slide before you. Let a nigga skate so much, he started thinking it was Cascades around this bitch. Please don't make me a single mom, Wiz."

"You won't ever have to worry about that cause I'm not going anywhere."

"Not voluntary. But if you play wit me, it'll be involuntary manslaughter. I've been through enough. I deserve the best."

"And that I plan to give you."

"Say you promise."

"I promise, beautiful."

The sincerity in his words matched his stare, and I believed him. I refused to let the past – whether it was in the form of a person or situation – dictate where our relationship was going.

I wanted to be happy. Wizdom made me happy. So, I wasn't going anywhere.

10

WIZDOM

"Bae, try this please. I promise it's not nasty." Lacey held out a hot Cheeto dipped in cream cheese that she'd been trying to convince me to eat for the last ten minutes.

Her red, stained fingers showed the damage she'd done to the two-ounce bag before trying to get me to be the test dummy for the chaos she called a craving. I'd been holding out thus far, but I knew I was on the losing end of the battle. Whether it was pickles and peanut butter, pickled asparagus, or most recently, hot Cheetos dipped in cream cheese, something always outnastied the other. Her face held mischief, and she wasn't backing down, still holding the chip up for me to bite.

"Beautiful, you killin' me. Ain't we supposed to be loving each other?" I smirked, leaning back on the couch and eyeing the Cheeto.

With a sly grin, she pulled the throw blanket off her body, revealing her now five-month-old round belly that poked out under my t-shirt she'd stole weeks ago. Climbing on top of me, she held the Cheeto in front of my face. Since moving in, she'd become more comfortable in my clothes than hers. I'd find shorts missing, hoodies, and even my sweats. And it didn't matter how many times I offered to get her her own; she'd always decline. Her excuse being wearing my clothes made her feel close to me when I wasn't home.

"Bae, it's so good. I swear." She tried coercing me. "Would I lie to you?"

"Yes." I laughed. "You lied to me about that nasty ass pickled asparagus. Then, you really took it to hell with the pickles and peanut butter. Your cravings taste buds are too crazy for my liking."

"Bae, pleaseeee."

I sighed like she was stressing me, but truth be told, I'd do just about anything for her. Especially after the last two months. The last two months were something different. Living with Lacey had changed my whole rhythm. Before, I was at her crib at least three days out of the week. Now, I slept with her curled up next to me every night. One hand usually held her belly like she was guarding a secret and the other under her head while I held them both.

The pregnancy had been going smooth so far. Our baby was growing, and each time we went to a doctor's appointment reassured Lacey that in just a few short months, she would be bringing our bundle of joy into the world. Her bout with morning sickness had subsided, allowing her to eat whatever made her heart content – in moderation. She had her moments of random tears when watching TV and even occasional mood swings, but I loved every moment of it. I loved her.

"Bae, open please." She pushed with the Cheeto now at my lip.

"Beautiful…"

"Wizdom. Just take a small bite. Don't make me cry, bae. This my last one, and I'm tryna share it witchu."

I snorted. "So, you gon' guilt trip me into eating the chip, beautiful? You know, some would call this emotional blackmail, right?"

"No. This is pregnancy," she shot back, grinning. "And if you love me like you say you do, you'll eat this. Here comes the choo choo train."

The first thing I tasted was the heat from the Cheeto, then the tangy cream cheese set in. The combination was weird for sure, but after letting the flavors kick in, it lowkey hit.

"Soooo?"

"It's aight," I admitted with a shrug. "I wouldn't eat it again."

"Told you it was good!" she said proudly, kissing my lips. "Me and baby would never steer you wrong. Ain't that right, baby?" She rubbed her belly and smiled.

Content that she'd managed to swindle me again, she curled up in my lap and rested her head on my shoulder. I rubbed her belly, thinking about how I'd been falling deeper in love with her every day. Moving in together was the best suggestion I could've made. She had a nigga taking midday naps when she felt I was doing too much and not getting adequate rest. She was teaching me how to cook, ensuring that I had something on my stomach before I left the house and a meal when I made it back in – no matter the time.

I thought pregnancy would make Lacey clingy, but she was chill so long as I made it back home every night. We'd settled into a routine that worked for us. It helped that we had no issues from the outside too. It seemed that both our exes had taken the hint to keep their distance, which was a good thing on their part.

"What time did Cherish say to be at her crib again?" I asked.

"8:30. And she said whoever's late and doesn't come with a basketful of their assigned color has to pay for the other couples' stuff that they bought in their basket. So, we gotta make sure we bring our receipt."

"What?" I chuckled. "Who agreed to that shit? She just made that up on the fly, didn't she?"

"Dropped it in the group text this morning. I don't know why we let her host, bae." She laughed.

"Me either. It's five o'clock now tho. You tryna saddle up for Daddy?"

"Can you eat my coochie first?"

Licking my lips, I nodded. "I sure can."

Pulling the shirt over her head, my mouth watered at the sight of her dark areolas. Her nipples hardened at my touch as I brushed my fingers across them before sucking the left one into my mouth.

"Ohhh," she crooned, throwing her head back.

My dick bricked up at her moaning. Making sure to give special attention to both titties, I gently pushed her back on the couch. The wet stain on the seat of her thong told me she wanted this dick as bad as it wanted her. Spreading her legs, I pulled the thong to the side, exposing a freshly waxed pussy waiting to be devoured. Positioning myself so that I was eye level, I flattened my tongue and swiped it up and down her slit.

"Just like that, bae," she coached, thrusting her hips upward to feed me the pussy.

Taking it as a challenge, I sucked on her clit while simultaneously sliding two fingers in her wet box. Watching her juices spill out of her while she moaned gave me instant gratification.

"Pussy so good. So pretty. So fucking fat." I praised between licks. "You gon' cum for Daddy?" I encouraged, spitting on her pussy and slurping it back up along with her clit.

"Oh, Goddd," she cried out, legs shaking.

"Not God, beautiful. Daddy. Ain't shit Godly bout this. Cum for Daddy." Homing in on her clit, I continued to flick my tongue up and down rapidly until she burst.

"Wizdommmmmm!"

I didn't stop licking until her body stopped shaking. "That's one. You need a minute?" I questioned through a smirk, watching her chest heave up and down.

"Nope. I'ma bout to show you a magic trick."

My dick jumped at the thought of her making it disappear. Pulling my shorts down to my ankles, it stood at attention. She swung her right leg over mine, held onto the back of the couch for leverage, and slowly slid down on my dick. I grabbed a handful of her ass with one hand and the back of her neck with the other.

"Ride that dick, Mama," I whispered in her ear before sinking my teeth into her neck.

Taking direction like a good girl, she bounced up and down and threw a little right swirl, left swirl combo that made my toes curl. She was doing that shit so good I had to grab her by her hips to keep her still while I thrust into her. I needed to control the motion to avoid cumming quick. That pregnant pussy was dangerous.

"Ooouuu, yessss," she moaned. "It feels so good, Dada. You feel so good inside of me. Sssss. You gon' make me cum."

Feeling myself about to nut, I spread her cheeks and sped up my strokes. I refused to get mine before she got hers at least twice. The pussy was so wet and warm, I had to zero in on the wall to keep from nutting quick.

"Gimme that shit, Alacea. I'm bout to bust. Wet that dick up for Daddy."

"Uhhhhh, right there, baby. I'm cummin'!"

"Shit! Me too." I held her hips in place and let her grind the nut out of me. "Let's stay home and tell Cherish the baby needed her rest."

She put her face in my neck and laughed. "Ain't no lets. If you wanna back out of the game night, you call Cherish and let her know."

"You call her for us. That's your girl."

"That's your sister," she countered.

"You scared." I tried the reverse psychology to see if she'd take the bait.

"No, nigga. I'm on to you. Yo' ass is scared."

Sucking my teeth, I moved my hips, making my dick jump inside her. "Ain't nobody scared. I just don't wanna hear her mouth. Come on, let's go take a shower."

"Exactly," she giggled. "I just put on one hell of a performance with this belly. You gotta carry me into the shower."

Seeing my dick coated in her juices as she climbed off me made me hard again.

"Wait, bae," I said, squeezing her thigh. "He won't go down. You gotta suck it."

"You so spoiled. Stand up."

Grinning, I stood and put two pillows behind her back. "Gotta make sure my baby comfortable when she giving up that good throat."

She sucked me up so good, I texted Cherish and asked her if she needed anything else for the night. A nigga was feeling generous.

What was supposed to be an hour nap after the shower turned into two hours, and we were now rushing to get out of the house. Well, Lacey was doing more of the rushing while I casually did a walkthrough, making sure everything was off and shut down.

"Wizdom, come on. Now you taking your time on purpose. We still gotta go to the store."

"Don't rush me, woman. You actin' like we bout to miss out on something. Somebody making a special appearance or something?"

"No, but this is Cherish and Suge's first game night as an official couple."

I stared at her, waiting for her to tell me the significance. "What that mean?"

She shoved me and laughed. "It means it's important to her. You irritating. Come on." She pushed me out the door and locked up.

Suge and Cherish had been an official couple for about a month now. Suge wasn't playing when she said that Cherish would either be with her or nobody. I didn't know the details of what had happened between her and Keyon. I just knew that he was gone. I was cool with that. I didn't have to worry about my sister with Suge. And my mother was happy that she was finally living in her truth. Whatever the hell that was.

"I gotta get my grapes while we out too, bae. I want the green ones. Don't let me forget please."

"Okay. I got you." Reaching over her, I carefully snapped her seatbelt in place, making sure to tug on it so that it rested on her belly – not too snug but secure. "Y'all good?"

"Yep."

"What color we got?"

"Blue. I had Ashlynn pick up a basket for us since I forgot. That pregnancy brain ain't no joke."

"Aight, cool. For the sake of time and you acting like the world is gonna end if we're late, we'll go to the supermarket closer to her house."

"That's fine."

We ended up at a Whole Foods down the block from Cherish's place. It was less crowded than I expected it to be for a Saturday evening, but that was a plus. It would make for easy shopping and an even easier check out.

"I think it'll be better if we split up, bae," Lacey suggested. "I'm gonna go get my fruit, and you can grab the blue stuff."

"Nah. Ain't no splittin' up. I leave you for ten minutes, and you guaranteed to come back with a cartful. I know you."

She snickered. "If you can't shop on your own, just say that you need Big Mama's help."

"Nah. Big Mama betta get that fruit and bring dat ass to the register." Placing a wet kiss on her lips, I smacked her ass and sent her on her way.

She didn't know it, but I was putting her on a timer. She had seven minutes to walk the aisles like I knew she would before grabbing what she actually wanted. Once it hit the ten-minute mark, I was going to find her. I hit the snack aisle first. Cherish had given us an A1 color. I knew I could find a bunch of shit. As I navigated the people, I found myself in the baby section. Looking at all the different brand of pampers, I thought about the gender reveal that we had planned at the end of the month.

I'd given Cherish the vision and put the planning in her hands alongside Ashlynn. I was adamant about Lacey not knowing any details because the sex of the baby wouldn't be the only surprise. Speaking of surprises, I hadn't received one screenshot of a receipt since I'd given Cherish a lumpsum of cash. Taking out my phone, I dialed her number.

"How far are y'all?" She answered on the second ring.

"Mommy raised you better than that, Bam."

"You right. Let me take a page out of her book. Hey. Where yo' black ass at, Wizdom?"

Chuckling, I pushed my cart out of the baby section to grab my remaining items. **"You sound just like her. We at the supermarket."**

"Oh, my God! So, nobody cares that I planned something nice for y'all stankin' asses and even cooked? Y'all foul."

"What you cooked, Bam?" I asked, knowing she didn't even like cooking.

"Food, nigga."

I cracked up. **"You all in an uproar knowing you paid somebody to cook whatever you got over there. I'm yo' brother. I know you."**

Sucking her teeth, she continued on her rant. "**That ain't the point. The point is I said 8:30. It's 9 o'clock. None of y'all are here. Not even Suge ugly ass. Talkin' bout she got caught up but on her way.**"

"**That's a real possibility tho, sis. We gon' be there in a minute. That ain't why I called. I called to find out the status of the gender reveal. I ain't seen not one receipt yet.**"

"**Things are getting done. I have receipts, but Im not bout to send pics every time, Wizdom. I'm documenting it all to hand you everything at once. Don't start that micro-managing.**"

"**Man, when it's...**" My other line beeped with a call from Lacey. "**Hold on. This my baby.**"

"**No. I'll see y'all when y'all get here.**"

Shaking my head, I clicked over to Lacey. "**I'm coming to find you.**"

"**I'm at self-checkout. Can you meet me here?**"

"**On my way. Stay on the phone.**" I picked up on her voice. She normally spoke in a soft tone. This was a little too soft. Almost nervous.

I pushed the cart up front and spotted her standing at the self-checkout line. Only she wasn't in the line. She stood stiff, next to the registers, watching the people like she was looking for someone.

"Who you looking for?" I questioned, ending the call once I was in front of her.

"Nobody," she replied, checking the items in the cart. "You did good. Come on."

I didn't say anything else as she placed her fruit in the cart and pushed it forward. I planned to address it in the car though. After scanning and bagging everything, we made our way out to the parking lot. I loaded the bags and situated her inside before asking what was up again.

"Quan was inside the store."

My jaw flexed. "That nigga say something to you?" I asked with my hand on the handle of the driver's side door.

"No. He didn't say anything. Just smiled and looked like he wanted to. He wouldn't have with the girl with him."

"What that nigga had on? And who was he with?"

"The girl from the park. And he had on an Amiri hoodie and hat. Why?"

"Say less."

Pulling out my phone, I hit Suge. The phone rang once before the call connected.

"Cherish, if this you calling from your brother phone, I'm still on my way like I told you three minutes ago, bae. Literally down the block. Bout to pass the Whole Foods."

"Aye, it's me."

"Oh, what's good?"

"I'm about to text you. Check yo' other phone and come to the Whole Foods." Ending the call, I sent Suge a message from my trap phone. "Did they have a cart? Like they were shopping?"

"Yes. Why?"

"Nothing. Let's get to Cherish's house, so we can show everybody who the better couple is around these parts."

My phone chimed with a response from Suge as I started the car.

Lacey didn't know it, but I was testing her. Had she even hesitated on answering my questions, I would've known she still had love for that nigga, Quan. Her responses had given me all the clarity I needed. I pulled out of the parking lot, knowing after tonight, that nigga was gon' be thinkin' about her from the grave.

121

11

ALACEA

"Aight, bae. This the last one before we take the W. You got this." Wizdom kissed my lips before sitting down in front of me while I stood in the middle of the living room.

We were in the middle of an intense game of Heads Up. The other couples had their turns, and so far, Wiz and I were down by a couple points. I needed to guess everything he described correctly in order to come out on top. Game night had really brought out my man's competitive side. So far, we'd won two out of the four games Cherish had set up, and he claimed that the ones we lost were rigged. I had to bring the win home for my baby.

"We need to put a limit on the amount of encouragement one partner can give the other," Keem argued from where he stood against the wall with his arms around Ashlynn's waist.

"Nigga," Wiz started, "ain't nobody say shit when you were whispering in Ashlynn ear."

"I wasn't whispering no encouraging words though. I was saying some nasty shit. I said if we take home this W, she can get this d…" Ashlynn smacked her hand over his mouth real quick before he could let the last word slip.

"Can y'all please take y'all turn?" She smiled, rolling her eyes.

"Alright." I giggled. "You ready, baby?"

Wizdom nodded with that little smirk that always sat on his lips, and I started the countdown. As soon as it hit one, he fired off descriptions like he was on a game show. Me and my man were locked in – we made a hell of a team. I was able to make out the correct answers with little effort on his part. And we were on a roll.

"Last one, bae. Ummm, your favorite position is?"

"Wizdom!"

Everybody laughed, but he didn't let up.

"Bae, forreal. We runnin' outta time. What's your favorite position?"

"Oh, my God… on top."

"Okay. And what you do to Daddy when you up there?"

"Ride."

"Okay, so you a rider, and then there's other professional riders like yourself. They be at the rodeo."

"Cowgirls?"

"Yep!"

Standing to his feet, he pulled me to him and smashed his lips into mine. "That's another W. High five, baby." We slapped fives like we'd just won a championship game.

"Y'all nasty," Cherish said, mushing him in the back of the head. "Let's eat before we get to the other games."

"Yo, Wiz," Suge called from across the room, giving him a head nod.

"Go head. I'm gonna make you a plate. A little bit of everything?"

"Yeah. Thanks, beautiful."

While he went over to see what Suge wanted, I made my way into the kitchen with the girls. Ashlynn and Cherish had plates lined up on the counter, ready to serve.

"Wiz is so out of line for that cowgirl description." Ashlynn laughed as I walked in.

"Right," Cherish agreed. "Talkin' bout, 'And what you be doing to Daddy while you up there?' Nasty ass."

Grinning, I made my way down the line. "I mean, he knows his woman. And Keem ain't no better."

"I think I might just really love that man," she admitted, taking me and Cherish by surprise.

"Think? Girl, y'all been loving each other," Cherish said. "Y'all just don't want us to know for whatever reason."

I nodded in agreeance, taking a bite of one of the hot honey wings.

"Just like you ain't want us to know that you and Suge have been a thing on the low until you made things official?" Ashlynn fired back.

"Ya right about that one," I egged on.

"That's only because Suge didn't want to openly be a thing with me while I was pretending like I was happy in a relationship with Keyon. I had to respect that and let her eat my coochie and dick me down in private. And her rule was that I couldn't get mad when I saw her with other chicks. I'm so glad that shit is over. Now, I have every right to cut her ass if she play wit me."

"A dick down from Suge sounds so crazy to me," I said.

"Shiiiddd, can't knock it 'til you try it, sis. Can't knock it 'til you try it." She sucked her bottom lip into her teeth and moaned.

"Girl, stop." Ashlynn threw a dish towel at her. "And she has tried it. We both have actually."

I twisted my lips up with a frown. "No, **we** have not."

"Lace, I was with a bitch name Tim, and you were with a bitch name Quan, remember?"

Cherish cracked up laughing. "You stupid. I'm over here looking dumb, tryna figure out what I missed."

"I gotta tell y'all something," I said, lowering my voice.

"Dammit, Lacey," Ashlynn stressed. "What the hell you done did?"

"Nothing. Calm down. I saw Quan tonight when we were at the supermarket. He was with that girl from the park."

"Really? Did you tell Wiz?" Cherish inquired.

"Yeah. I waited until we were in the car before I did though. I didn't want him to go crazy in the place."

"Right," Ashlynn agreed. "Too many witnesses."

Cherish crossed her arms. "What he say in the car?"

"He asked me if Quan said anything to me. I told him he didn't, and then he called Suge. He also asked about what Quan had on."

"Did you tell him?"

"Yeah. I wanted to pry and ask why he wanted to know, but my gut told me to just leave it alone."

"Glad you went with that," Ashlynn stated with a nod. "Let him handle it how he sees fit."

"You right." Cherish didn't say anything, but I caught her eye shift over to where Suge and Wizdom stood, talking off in a corner.

"Let's get these plates together, so we can eat and get back to it," she said. "We're doing the best basket contest next."

"Wait, who's judging? Cause you and Suge got a basket too. Y'all not bout to cheat us."

"I'ma call Dooty on FaceTime, so he can be the judge."

"Oh, then I already won." Ashlynn claimed the victory.

"Girl, please. Need I remind you that I'm Dooty's favorite?" I challenged.

"Aye, Delusional one and two." Cherish pointed to us. "In the living room so y'all can watch me win."

Stepping back into the living room, the guys were all seated, talking amongst themselves.

"Here you go, handsome face." I handed Wiz his plate and sat down next to him.

"Thank you, baby. Now, rest your feet. I've been watching you move around with my baby all night. I ain't say nothing cause I know you're having a good time. But sit down for a sec."

As if he or she were agreeing with Daddy, I felt a kick in my side. "Well, okay. The lil' person in charge just kicked me. I guess I have no choice but to listen." Rubbing my belly, I smiled. He placed his hand over mine and received his own kick.

"See, beautiful jr. already know who side to be on."

"Whatever."

For the next couple hours, we ate, talked shit, and clowned each other about the earlier games. We played two more, only these two, Cherish and Suge decided to sit out of, making it a two on two. She kept walking around with a whistle she'd found of Dooty's, blowing it in Keem's ear every time he tried to bend a rule or question one to work in his and Ashlynn's favor.

"Blow it again and I'ma beat yo' ass, Cherish," he threatened, covering his ear.

"Stop cheating then," she shot back, laughing.

"Cheating and getting caught," Suge added.

"Oh, you already actin' like an opp. Yo, bruh," he said to Wiz, "take her off payroll immediately."

Suge grinned. "A man is nothing without his right hand."

"Wanna be John Wick headass," Keem joked, and Wiz and Suge laughed.

By the end of the night, Keem and Ash had won one game, and me and Wiz had the other. We had to hold off on picking a winner for the basket. When Cherish called Dooty's phone on FaceTime, his mom picked up and let us know he was sleep. She was polite about it too. I was glad because I could tell by Cherish's face that she was waiting for her to say something wrong.

"Hey, you," I spoke from behind Wizdom when I found him outside on the balcony. Everyone had begun cleaning up, and he had disappeared. "You hidin'?" I teased, stepping out next to him.

"Nah. Just needed a minute to breathe. Night been fun as hell. We haven't gotten together to chill like this since Dooty birthday party."

"A.k.a., the best day of your life." I cheesed. I stood up on my tiptoes and kissed his cheek.

"One of them. The second was when we found out about this." Placing both hands on my belly, he turned me around so that my back was to him, and his head rested in the crook of my neck. "Crazy to think that we'll be meeting her in a few months."

We rocked slowly back-and-forth, taking in the night sky. My mind subconsciously wandered back to earlier.

"I'm glad we didn't let anything ruin tonight," I said softly.

"You talkin' bout the Quan situation?"

I nodded. "Yeah. I didn't know how you were going to react. I just didn't want you to lose your cool in there."

"I get it. But I am glad you said something. We're moving forward though." He kissed my neck. "And niggas like Quan... well, we'll let the universe deal with niggas like Quan."

Tilting my head, I looked up at him. "Agreed. You ready to go home?"

"Mmmhmm. Think you can climb down the balcony so Cherish don't see us leaving and we haven't helped clean up?"

"Let's just use the baby card this time."

"I love when you're onboard with being trifling witcho man."

"I love you too. We'll Cash App her later."

Walking back into the house, Suge, Ashlynn, and Keem were talking but no Cherish. Making a break for the front door, we left out, cracking up as we made our way to the car. I didn't mind dealing with Cherish later. I could take on anything and anyone with my partner in crime.

———

I ROLLED OVER, STRETCHING MY ARM ACROSS THE BED, EXPECTING the warmth of Wizdom's body to be there, but it wasn't. My eyes fluttered open slowly, looking over at the clock that read 6:15 a.m. I sat up, rubbing my belly, trying to blink the fog out of my mind. Then, it came to me, his voice whispering to me in the middle of the night when I was barely awake.

"Bae... I gotta handle somethin'. I'll be back in a few hours. I love you."

I remembered reaching for him to give me a kiss. I was half out of it but up enough to know that I wanted to feel his lips before he left. He pressed his lips against mine, then my cheek, and my forehead last. I mumbled for him to be safe before falling back out. But now, I was fully awake. And something didn't feel right. My stomach felt queasy. Swinging my legs over the edge of the bed, I grabbed my phone off the nightstand. There were no missed calls or texts. I went to dial his number, but my phone lit up with an incoming call from an unknown number.

I ignored it. If the number was unknown, then the person on the other end didn't need to speak to me. The phone lit up again. Unknown number danced across the screen. The baby kicked, and I took that as a sign. *Please, God, don't let this be bad news,* I thought to myself.

I answered with shaky hands. **"Hello?"**

An automated voice came through on the other end. **"You are receiving a collect call from... Wizdom... an inmate at Metropolitan Correctional Center. Do you accept the charges?"**

My breath got caught in my throat as I went to answer. **"Y-yes."**

There was brief static before his voice came through clearly. **"Baby, take a deep breath. Don't panic. I'm okay."**

Tears stung my eyes instantly. **"Wizdom... baby... what's going on? What hap..."**

"**I need you to listen to me first,**" he cut in gently. "**Cherish and Ashlynn are on their way to you right now. They should be there any minute. I'm good, baby. I was picked up for questioning. I can't go into the details right now but know that I'm okay, aight?**"

My heart pounded as I gripped the phone tight to keep it from slipping. "**I don't understand. Questioning for what, Wizdom?**"

"**Alacea,**" he called my name, firm but soft. "**You gotta breathe, beautiful. Breathe and stay calm for the baby. Need you to do that for me. I'll see you soon.**"

The automated message announced thirty more seconds in the call.

I choked back a sob, blinking fast. "**Okay. I love you.**"

"**I love you too, beautiful. More than anything. I gotta go, but I'ma ca...**"

The call disconnected at the same time I heard a hard knock at the front door. I couldn't even bring myself to get up. I had to let everything sink in for a second. The knock came again. Wiping my face, I stood to my feet and slowly walked out front. Unlocking the door with shaky hands, I pulled it open and stepped back.

Cherish and Ashlynn stood there, faces tight with worry and sadness. I had no words, just gestured with my hand for them to come inside.

"He just called," I said once they were inside. "A collect call... said he was picked up for questioning but couldn't tell me why over the phone." I looked at Cherish. "Why couldn't he tell me? What is it that he can't say over the phone?"

Her bottom lip quivered before she bit it.

"Please," I begged. "Just tell me."

Ashlynn looked to Cherish like she needed to be the one to say it.

Wiping her eyes fast, Cherish took a deep breath. "They're charging him, Lace."

"I'm beginning to understand that now, Cherish," I said, trying to hold back my frustration. "But with what?"

"Quan's murder," Ashlynn answered for her.

"Quan's what? No. Wizdom didn't kill no Quan. He was…"

"We know that, Lacey," Cherish spoke. "But they seem to believe that he did."

It felt like the walls were closing in.

"Suge called. The cops picked Wiz up while they were out. Supposedly, his name was mentioned in connection with it."

"When the hell did all this happen? He didn't kill anyone. He was with us last night, and we fell asleep together. This shit don't make sense!"

"Quan was killed last night," Ashlynn confirmed. "Hit up while he was in his car."

"This is not happening right now." I covered my mouth as tears poured down my cheeks. "He didn't do that shit."

They both embraced me, holding me tight to prevent me from falling. They wanted me to be strong for the baby, but this was bad. All bad.

12

ALACEA

The last few weeks had been hell on me mentally. My life had literally flipped upside down on me overnight. One minute, I was lying in bed under my man, feeling him rub my belly and whisper how grateful he was for me and our baby... then the next, I was sitting in a courtroom, stomach doing somersaults, hearing a judge tell him he was being held without bond. Those words shattered my heart. What hurt the most was that there was nothing I could do but pray. Wiz kept his head held high that day. And every day since then, reminding me that the situation was temporary whenever he called.

And here I was, weeks later, barely holding it together. I was trying to be strong for him. For us. For the little life growing inside of me. But that shit was easier said than done. The pregnancy became much harder, and I knew it was due to me being so down in the dumps. I slept a lot, but rest was the key, and I didn't get much of that. The house felt cold, even with everyone on a constant rotation, checking on me.

Every doctor's appointment ended with me in tears, despite

the family documenting the moments. It wasn't the same without him being physically present.

And today? Today was the gender reveal. One he was still excited for. One he refused to let us cancel although he knew that he wouldn't be here to celebrate with us. And if he couldn't celebrate it, I didn't want to. I couldn't bring myself to smile, take pictures, and laugh when my man was sitting behind bars.

Sitting on the edge of the bed in my robe and a headscarf, I stared at my phone in my hand, waiting for his call. Out in the living room, I heard my mom, Ms. Angela, Ashlynn, and Cherish moving around. They'd come over this afternoon, dressed to the nines in their different shades of pink and blue. While they thought I was in my room getting ready, I had yet to get up from the spot I'd been sitting in since getting out of the shower. My eyes were puffy from crying damn near all night. The more I thought about Wiz, the more I wanted to cry.

A soft knock at the bedroom door pulled my attention.

"Lacey," I heard Ms. Angela call to me. "You okay, honey?"

I cleared my throat to answer. "Trying to be."

"Is it okay if I come in?"

"Yes." She opened the door and came inside. "Oohh, baby girl. You've been in here crying the whole time?" she asked, sitting down next to me and wrapping her arm around my shoulder. "Wizdom would not want you like this. Especially on this special day."

"It doesn't feel special without him. At all."

"And I get that, honey. But…"

My phone rang in my hand, interrupting her. I held the phone up. "It's him." Answering on speakerphone, I let the automated system do its thing and immediately accepted the call.

"**Hey, beautiful.**" His voice came through strong. "**You ready for today?**"

"**No, she is not,**" his mother answered for me. "**She been in here crying. She needs to hear you.**"

"Aight, Ma. I got it. Thank you."

"Okay. I love you." She kissed my forehead and got up to leave the room.

"Baby. You there?"

"Yes."

"I need you to go to the reveal. I need you to go for me. For our baby."

I shook my head, tears spilling. "It's gonna hurt even more to be there without you."

"I know, baby. Trust me, I'm fucked up about it too. But our family worked hard on this, and our lil' girl," he paused, "she deserves them memories. You don't gotta fake smile for nobody. Just be there for us. Hold it down. I need you to do that for me. Please."

Wiping my face, I nodded. "Okay. I'll go."

"That's my girl. Gimme kiss."

I made a kissing sound in the phone and smiled lightly. "I miss you."

"I miss you too, baby. And I love you. Go show up and show out for us."

When the call ended, I sat there for a second. Inhaling deeply, I exhaled and got up to get dressed. If my man was strong enough to tell me to celebrate, the least I could do was honor that. Honor him and the life we'd created.

———

The gender reveal was held at a beautiful two-story house in Yonkers. When we pulled up, my mouth damn near fell open. The driveway was lined with pink and blue balloons and a custom banner that read, A CELEBRATION FIT FOR A PRINCE OR PRINCESS in bold, gold letters. The whole place was decked out. Light pink and baby blue satin was draped along the walls. There were huge flower arrangements everywhere inside the house as we walked through. A "Mommy & Daddy to be" table sat off in the corner with place settings to match the décor.

From the candy bar to the personalized cookies with onesies on them and the photobooth, I found myself choked up. Cherish came over to me and hugged me tight.

"He made us promise not to cancel, no matter what you said," she said in my ear. "He wanted you to see everything he planned and for you to know that you still deserved a celebration even in his absence."

I nodded, feeling my throat tighten again as she pulled away. "Thank you."

"No problem, sista. We got each other. No matter what." We embraced again briefly, and she went to check on the guests.

I really didn't want to be bothered but made sure I mingled for a few, wanting everyone to know that I appreciated them. Music played, we ate, and the photobooth had a continuous line of people wanting to capture the moment. I shuffled between my mom, Wizdom's mom, and the girls to lean on for strength throughout the celebration. Each one of them gave me what I needed to get through the day.

Before I knew it, the DJ announced that it was time for the reveal. Everybody gathered outside on the patio where there was a huge gold balloon hanging from an arch wrapped in pink and blue tulle.

"Alright, y'all," Cherish spoke into the mic, "Wiz and Lacey left me in charge, so don't have me out here looking crazy. On three, Lacey is gonna pop the balloon, and we gon' find out if we're having a little prince or princess."

"Wait, bae." Suge walked out from the crowd with an iPad in her hand. "My bad, y'all. We can't do this without my boy." I stood there just as confused as the family. Then, it became clear when she handed me the iPad, and Wizdom's face popped up.

"**Wassup, beautiful?**" He spoke with a smile so big and infectious; I showed all of my pearly whites.

"**Hi, handsome face.**" I spoke through fresh tears. I looked over at Cherish, who was crying as well.

"**Let me see everybody real quick.**" I flipped the camera, and the crowd let out a wave of hey's and I love you's. Cherish walked over, putting the mic at the speaker. "**Wassup, y'all? Come on, bae. Let's do this reveal.**"

Handing the iPad to Suge to hold where he could see, I stood under the balloon with the little pin they handed me and waited for the countdown.

"One… two… three!"

I popped the balloon, and a huge cloud of soft pink confetti burst out, floating down all around me. Everybody cheered. I looked over at the screen, and Wiz just nodded and grinned. A little girl. Our little princess.

"Wait, there's more," Cherish announced. "Tell her, bro."

"**Alacea, a child can be raised anywhere so long as that child is surrounded by love. But I want us to raise our baby right here. In this home, in this very backyard. Welcome home, baby.**"

"**Wizdom! No, you didn't!**"

"Yes, he did! This yo' new house, boo!" Cherish exclaimed.

The family erupted again in cheer while I took the iPad and walked off to the side, needing a private moment.

"**I love you so much. When did you have time to do all this?**" I asked in awe.

"**I do things.**" He smirked. "**I've been working on this before all this shit went down. I had to make it perfect for my girls.**"

I tilted the iPad so that he could see my stomach. "**Well, this little girl will know how much her daddy loves her.**"

"**She damn sure will. And as soon as I'm outta here, we**

gon' fill that house with so much love she ain't gon' know nothin' but that."

"We waiting on you."

"I'll be there soon. I promise. I love you, Alacea."

"I love you more, Wizdom."

"Go finish celebrating. This my phone, so I'll call later."

"Okay, baby. Talk soon."

We hung up, and for the first time since he'd been gone, I felt a little relief. How he got a phone in prison, I didn't know and didn't care to know. What I did know was we were going to make it through this. Me, him, and our baby girl.

13

WIZDOM

Four months.

I'd been locked up in this motherfucka for four long ass months without a bond. I ain't gon' lie. That first month, I thought them people were just getting they shit off. When month two rolled around and still no word about bond, I almost lost it. Never in my life did I think I'd be sitting in a cell, staring at concrete walls every day, listening to broke niggas talk about what they planned to do once they got out. All because a judge ain't have shit better to do the day my case hit his docket but be a dickhead.

At first, I was tight. All I could think about was my woman sitting at home with our baby growing inside of her, going through the hardest part of her pregnancy without me. Of course, we had our village, but she needed me. Shit ain't sit right on my chest at all. When month two went by, I realized I had two choices – sit here and fold or go to war for my freedom. I could never fold. A nigga had too much to lose. So, I went to war alongside my family and an A1 lawyer.

I sent word through Suge to my contact, Peace, and he put me on to his lawyer without any questions. He also put a play together that got me a phone after my first couple weeks in. The phone became my lifeline to the outside. Every day, I faced the screen, watching Lacey's belly grow in real time. It was as good as good could get since I blocked everyone from coming to visit. As much as I missed them, I couldn't stomach my people coming up to the jail to see me.

So, we kept it to FaceTime and phone calls. Suge had been holding me down heavy. She kept the blocks moving and kept me updated on everything, even stuff I didn't care to know. She made sure the paper was right with my lawyer to ensure no delays in working on my behalf too. And my lawyer was worth every dollar I put in his pocket. He picked apart my case from every angle. It was clear through the shoddy police work and weak evidence that they were trying to pin Quan's murder on me because of my connection with Lacey with no real evidence.

Did I put in the call to have his bitch ass knocked off? Of course I did. That didn't stop my lawyer from filing motions on my behalf and staying on the judge's neck. He was earning his pay, and eventually... the motions started sticking. Last week, when I heard him say that there was a real chance that I'd be home in time for my daughter's birth, I almost shed a tear. All I wanted was to be there for my girls. I prayed every night for that chance.

And today? That chance came. My lawyer came through and got me processed out on a $50,000 bond to which I covered without blinking an eye. The process wasn't drawn out. And when I made it outside, Suge and Keem were waiting on me. I made it clear that I didn't want anyone else to know that I was being released. I wanted it to be a surprise.

"Rickyyyyyyy!" Suge yelled out, making me laugh as I made it to the car.

"You stupid."

"Welcome home, man." She hugged me, and Keem followed.

"Wassup, bruh? Come on and get in."

I got in on the passenger side, while Suge got in the back, with Keem taking the driver's seat. "Dawg, I'm ready to get the hell home. Y'all didn't tell anybody, did you?"

"Only my reflection in the mirror," Suge said.

"Your surprise is safe, my boy," Keem confirmed.

"Cool. I blocked Lacey and sold that phone in there after I erased it. You got that Cash App, right, Suge?"

"Yep."

Opening my property bag, I checked for my phone. Pulling it out, I went to power it on, but it was dead.

"You wanna grab something to eat on our way or go straight home?" Keem inquired.

"Home. I'll eat there."

"Hold on, shhh. This Cherish," Suge said, answering her phone. **"Wassup, bae?"**

"Lacey's in labor. We're in St. Mary's. I can't get Wizdom on the phone at the number he gave us. She can't either. Can you try to call? This girl over here talkin' bout she ain't pushing until she speak to him."

Suge handed me the phone without me having to ask for it. **"Which St. Mary's, Bam?"**

"Wizdom?"

"Yes. Which St. Mary's?"

"Oh, shit. The one by your condo. When you..."

"I'll tell you later. Don't tell her I'm on my way. If she wants to wait, let her wait, but if them doctors say she gotta push, make her push. You got me?"

"Yeah. I got you. Welcome home, bro. I love you."

"Love you too." I hung up and gave Suge back her phone. "Drive this shit, Keem."

139

WE MADE IT TO THE HOSPITAL, AND I HOPPED OUT BEFORE KEEM could make a full stop. Rushing through the front doors like my life depended on it, I went right up to the front desk.

"Sir…" the receptionist started.

"Labor and delivery unit please."

"It's on the third floor, sir. Is there someone I can look up for you?"

"Yes. Alacea Smith."

"Are you a family member, friend?"

"Father of the child she's about to deliver."

"Oh, congratulations. Do you have your ID?"

"It's in my car. Miss, can we handle this in a few? I need to get upstairs."

"Here's his ID." Suge came through yet again, handing my ID to the lady. I looked over at her, and she nodded. "I know, nigga. You'll lose your shit if there was no me. Go up there and have a baby."

"Love you, dawg."

"I know. Love you too."

Passing the elevators, I took the steps up to the third floor. I gave Lacey's name at the receptionist desk there, and they pointed me to room 3201. Pushing the door to the room open, the sight in front of me almost brought me to my knees. There my lady was, laying there, breathing heavy, looking exhausted but beautiful as hell. As soon as she saw me, her eyes widened before the tears came.

"Look who made it," her mom said, smiling big.

"You made it." Lacey's voice cracked once I was at her side.

I kissed her forehead and grabbed her hand. "I'm here, baby. Daddy's home."

Still crying, she squeezed my hand. "She waited for you."

I looked down at her belly, tears spilling from my own eyes now. "We're ready for you, Justice."

Dr. Mallory entered, all gowned up. "Perfect timing, Dad. We're ready to push. You ready, Lacey?"

She looked up at me and nodded. "I'm ready," she replied with confidence, setting her feet up in the stirrups.

"Okay. Grandma, I'm going to have you grab one leg, and Daddy, you grab the other. Lacey, on the next contraction, I want you to push."

Minutes felt like hours, but finally on the sixth push and one final war cry, the room filled with the sounds of our daughter's wails. It was music to my ears.

"Here's your baby girl," Dr. Mallory said, placing her on Lacey's chest.

She was perfect with a headful of dark curls, little chubby cheeks, and was loud as hell.

"Hi, Justice," Lacey whispered. "Hi, baby. Look at you Daddy. He made it home to see you."

I kissed Lacey's lips and Justice's forehead. "I'll always make it home to y'all. No matter what."

EPILOGUE

ONE YEAR LATER

"Aight, Jus, you gotta work wit Daddy this morning and let me get these ponytails right. There's bragging rights on the line and a month full of... Well, you don't need to know that part. Just sit still for me."

I sat on the floor in Justice's room, struggling with two rubber bands and an active toddler who could give a damn about the bet me and her mom made last night. My baby girl was officially one now – a whole twelve months of life, light, and loud giggles that filled every inch of our house. She was a little busybody, always on the go and looking for an adventure.

"Aight, you got it." I laughed, pulling her onto my lap and kissing her chubby cheeks. "You wanna walk around wit your hair all wild, Daddy gon' let you do you."

"Looks like I won the bet," Lacey said from the doorway. She stood, leaned up against the frame, smiling with her arms crossed and a glow about her that you couldn't miss. "You a tough guy out there but a big softie with her. You supposed to make her sit, so you can do her hair. Like I do."

"Nah, that's your role. Remember, you bad cop, and I'm super daddy. Right, Jus?" I tickled her, and she laughed.

Strutting over to us in one of my tees and a pair of shorts that were barely hanging on, she bent down in front of me to pick Justice up. "Come on, mami. Let me do ya hair and make you pretty."

"Pwetty," Justice repeated.

"That's right," I concurred. "Just like Mommy." I smacked Lacey on the ass as I stood.

"Tsk. Tsk. And you lost that bet."

I thought about the bet we made to let me get that bootyhole the whole month and shook my head. "A good fiancée would still let me get in there anyway."

"Boy, please." Sitting Justice down in her chair, she squatted and began to expertly brush her hair up into two ponytails with no problem. "See, this takes skills right here." She kissed Justice's cheek and picked her up from the chair. "Let's go get lunch, pretty girl."

Justice clapped and giggled like she understood what was going on.

My heart couldn't take this shit sometimes. Just a year ago, I was in court, fighting a body, and now, by the grace of God, I woke up to this every day. The prosecution had fucked up so bad with my case, they had to drop the charges on me when the witness they claimed they had just dropped off the face of the earth. Once again, the odds worked in my favor. Kinda like how me and Lacey came to be.

"Aye," I said to Lacey as she strapped Justice in her highchair.

She turned back to me. "Wassup?"

"You know a gangsta love you, right?"

"Mmmhmm. I do. And I love a gangsta."

The End

& Y'ALL KNOW HOW THIS WORKS. SAY IT WIT ME...

I DON'T WANNA ARGUE!

Did you enjoy the read?
Let us know how much by leaving us a
review on Amazon and Goodreads.

145

ALSO BY NAI

A Secret Love Affair With The Plug

Wrapped Up In A Hitta's Love For Christmas

Yours For The Taking

Seizing A Gangsta's Heart For The Summer

Thug Me The Right Way

Thug Me The Right Way 2

Thug Me The Right Way 3

A Summer To Remember With My Hitta

Snatched Up By A Hitta

Wet Dreams On Lockdown: The Unit Manager

Santa Sent Me A Real One For Christmas

Bossin' Up On The Plug

Bossin' Up On The Plug 2

In The Trenches With My Hitta

In The Trenches With My Hitta 2

Stealing A Queenpin's Heart

Stealing A Queenpin's Heart 2

A Piece of A Hustler's Heart

A Piece of A Hustler's Heart 2

A Thug's Love Mended My Heart

A Thug's Love Mended My Heart 2

A Summer To Remember With My New York Bae

A Summer Fling In New York

His Hood Love Gave Me Life

His Hood Love Gave Me Life 2

My Thug, My Sanctuary

Thug Kisses For Christmas

For The Love Of My Savage

Charge It To The Game

Charge It To The Game 2

Charge It To The Game 3

OTHER BOOKS BY

URBAN AINT DEAD

Tales 4rm Da Dale

The Hottest Summer Ever

Hittin' Licks For The Holidays: Atlanta

Wet Dreams On Lockdown: The Nurse

How To Publish A Book From Prison

How To Invest In The Stock Market From Prison

By **Elijah R. Freeman**

Despite The Odds

Despite The Odds 2

By **Juhnell Morgan**

Good Girls Gone Rogue

Good Girls Gone Rogue 2

By **Manny Black**

Hittaz

Hittaz 2

Hittaz 3

Hittaz 4

Hittaz 5

Hittaz 6

Coldhearted

Coldhearted 2

Coldhearted 3

By **Lou Garden Price, Sr.**

Charge It To The Game

Charge It To The Game 2

Charge It To The Game 3

A Summer To Remember With My Hitta

Snatched Up By A Hitta

Santa Sent Me A Real One For Christmas

Wet Dreams On Lockdown: The Unit Manager

Thug Me The Right Way 2

Thug Me The Right Way 3

Seizing A Gangsta's Heart For The Summer

Yours For The Taking

Wrapped Up In A Hitta's Love For Christmas

By **Nai**

A Set Up For Revenge

A Set Up For Revenge 2

Wet Dreams On Lockdown: The Librarian

By **Ashley Williams**

Trickin' On A Heaux For Christmas

Homie Hoppin' For The Holidays

Wet Dreams On Lockdown: The Female C.O

Letters Of His Love

By **Telia Teanna**

The State's Witness

The State's Witness 2

The State's Witness 3

This Time Won't You Save Me

This Time Won't You Save Me 2

His Summer Side Piece

A Holiday Heist

Healing The Heart Of A Detroit Gangsta

The Promissory

By **Kyiris Ashley**

Stuck In The Trenches

Stuck In The Trenches 2

By **Huff Tha Great**

Melted The Heart Of A Menace

Wet Dreams On Lockdown: Lieutenant Grace

By **P. Wise**

Merry Trapmas

By **Mia Sky**

Thug Me The Right Way

By **DiamondATL & Nai**

Wet Dreams On Lockdown: The Counselor

By **Paris Iman**

Wet Dreams On Lockdown: The Male C.O

By **Tamyra Griffin**

Wet Dreams On Lockdown: The Captain

By **TN Jones**

Wet Dreams On Lockdown: The Warden

By **Shawnice**

Atlantastan

Atlantastan 2

By **Chris Green**

IN The Streetz

IN The Streetz 2

IN The Streetz 3

IN The Streetz 4

IN The Streetz 5

By **Tron Hill**

Hittin' Licks For The Holidays: New York

Bandemic

By **Freshh Moneyy**

Coming Soon From
URBAN AINT DEAD

Drill
The Hottest Summer Ever 2
THE G-CODE
Tales 4rm Da Dale 2
How To Build Your Credit From Prison
By **Elijah R. Freeman**

Good Girls Gone Rogue 3
By **Manny Black**

Despite The Odds 3
By **Juhnell Morgan**

A Felon's Promise
By **Nai**

Summer Vows With A Detroit Gangsta
The Promissory 2
By **Kyiris Ashley**

Atlantastan 3
By **Chris Green**

IN The Streetz 6
By **Tron Hill**

Bandemic 2
By **Freshh Moneyy**